Ties Can]

Sage Gardens Cozy Mystery Series

Cindy Bell

Copyright © 2015 Cindy Bell

All rights reserved.

All rights reserved. No part of this publication may be reproduced or transmitted in any form or by any means, electronic or mechanical, including photocopy, recording, or any information storage or retrieval system, without permission in writing from the publisher.

This is a work of fiction. The characters, incidents and locations portrayed in this book and the names herein are fictitious. Any similarity to or identification with the locations, names, characters or history of any person, product or entity is entirely coincidental and unintentional.

All trademarks and brands referred to in this book are for illustrative purposes only, are the property of their respective owners and not affiliated with this publication in any way. Any trademarks are being used without permission, and the publication of the trademark is not authorized by, associated with or sponsored by the trademark owner.

ISBN-13: 978-1517560287

ISBN-10: 1517560284

Table of Contents

Chapter One 1

Chapter Two 17

Chapter Three 30

Chapter Four 47

Chapter Five 61

Chapter Six 89

Chapter Seven 108

Chapter Eight 122

Chapter Nine 135

Chapter Ten 159

Chapter Eleven 168

Chapter Twelve 184

Chapter Thirteen 194

Chapter Fourteen 218

Chapter Fifteen 241

Chapter Sixteen 251

Chapter One

Eddy fumbled with his wallet. His thumbs were a source of frustration. It was as if they had lost some of their sensation over the years. When he tried to use them they tended to fail him. With a grunt of disapproval he managed to get his license out of his wallet. The young brunette behind the desk knew him by sight, but he didn't like to be treated differently. He knew the rules said that he had to show his identification when he withdrew funds, so that was what he did, every single time. Perhaps it was his past career as a police detective that made him such a stickler. He just felt rules were rules for a reason. Of course when he was wearing a badge he didn't always feel that way.

There were four people in line ahead of Eddy. He had waited for at least twenty minutes so far. His right knee ached. He shifted his feet and tapped his driver's license against his palm. It was unusual that there was only one teller at the desk at midday on a Friday. He would have avoided the bank rush hour, but whenever he visited in the past the line moved quickly.

Eddy considered himself a patient man. Others had commented on his short temper over the years, but he never really bought it. He got angry when the situation demanded it. If people would do what they were supposed to he wouldn't get so angry. Now he was losing his patience. Not because he had to wait so long, but because the brunette behind the desk looked frazzled. Eddy had been served by her many times and she was always very courteous. It was clear from the tension in her expression that she was very stressed by the fact that she was alone with so many customers to deal with. People began to grumble and complain.

The pretty, young woman looked as if she might cry. It really bothered Eddy when he saw someone being treated unfairly. He glanced around the bank in search of another teller. He noticed that there were three men in a glass-walled office to the side of the desk. The office was behind a secure door. He glared through the glass as if his displeasure could be communicated through the heaviness of his stare. He thought about waving to the men to try and get their attention. Then he noticed a gleam of something in one of the men's hands. At first he thought his eyes had to be tricking him. Maybe he was seeing something that wasn't there. What were the chances that he could be right about what he thought that was? Then he looked back at the brunette behind the counter. She looked past all of the other customers, straight to him. She met his eyes. Eddy stared at her for a long moment. She shook her head just enough for him to see. He knew then that he was right.

The gleam that he saw was the barrel of a gun. The reason why there weren't more tellers at the desk was because the bank was in the middle of a hold-up. Eddy had investigated his share of those during his career as a police officer. However, he had never come across one where the bank continued to function as if it was a regular business day. It was genius really. The robbers could be in and out without anyone suspecting a thing. By the time the alarm was set off there wouldn't be a chance of the police catching them.

Eddy felt his chest tighten with rage. All he wanted to do was take out a little cash to buy Samantha a birthday present. Instead he was thrust into the midst of a bank robbery. How could he ignore that? All of the grumbling people in line ahead of him were in grave danger. All of the bank employees were as well. He couldn't just ignore that.

The person in the front of the line finally completed his transaction. He turned around and walked out of the bank. Eddy tried to catch his attention. He was going to mention to the man to alert the authorities, but the man refused to even look in his direction. That was how it was in modern times, no one even bothered to look at each other. It irked Eddy, but he didn't have time to dwell on it. He knew that things could change, and fast. As long as there was an armed robber inside the bank anything could happen. He looked around at the other people in line and tried to make eye contact to see if any of them were concerned. He thought about turning around and leaving to get help, but he didn't want to leave these people alone.

Eddy's heart began to pound. He presumed that he was the only customer who had noticed what was happening in the glass office. His gaze swept the line in front of him. The potential hostages were great. An elderly woman, a man with a young boy hanging on his hand, and a young woman likely not yet in her twenties. Eddy looked back at the glass office. The man holding the gun had his back to the glass. Eddy couldn't tell much about him aside from his build. The other men in the room looked a little frantic. Whatever they were discussing was escalating quickly.

For a split second Eddy thought about

drawing his weapon. But then he remembered that he didn't have his gun anymore. He wanted to do something, but he did not want to put anyone at risk. If he tried something and it didn't work bullets might start flying and people were going to die. The father and son were at the front of the line now. Eddy could hear the little boy pleading for a lollipop. Then he heard the sound of the door on the glass office opening. The armed man stepped out behind the desk. His face was obscured by a cap and dark glasses. He raised his weapon for all to see.

"Lock that door!" He barked at the security guard.

Eddy's head spun. He had hoped that things would end peacefully, but it was clear from the anger in the robber's voice that something had gone wrong. Eddy wasn't sure what to do next. He could confront the robber and risk people getting hurt, or he could obey his commands.

"All of you, on the ground with your hands in the air. No funny business." He pointed the gun at the people in line. The little boy giggled as if he thought it was a game. His father cupped his hand around his mouth and pulled him down to his knees beside him. Eddy got angry, this was a moment the little boy might never forget. He glared at the robber. The pretty teller behind the counter met his eyes again. This time there were tears in hers. Eddy tried to think of how he could subdue the robber. He knew he had to be smart about the situation and not let his temper override his caution.

"Do you want me to hurt these people?" The robber waved his gun around as he directed his question to one of the men that had come out of the office. "All you have to do is give me the money." The man who the robber was talking to looked scared. "Now!"

Eddy was struck by the fact that there appeared to be only one robber. In his experience bank robbers almost always worked with partners, many times in groups. The fact that there was only one armed man made him very vulnerable. But Eddy could tell that he was also intelligent. He remained very close to the little boy. If Eddy tried something the boy might get hurt. Eddy gritted his teeth. He placed his wallet that he still held in his hand on the floor beside him. He kept his gaze focused on the teller behind the counter. She was shaking like a leaf caught in a windstorm, but she held back her tears. Eddy wished he understood how to use his cell phone better. He might be able to discretely call for help.

As the bank robber held up his gun the bank manager said in a trembling voice, "Please, don't hurt anyone."

"Like I said just get me all of the cash. No dye packs. All I want is money. Nobody has to die." He punctuated his words by pointing his gun directly at the bank manager's head. The man grimaced and nodded. Once the money had been collected, Eddy's gut twisted. He knew if the man was going to shoot, now would be the time. He instinctively slid his hand up his hip to where his gun would have been holstered, but there was no gun there.

"Like I said, nobody has to die. Just let me leave." He stepped out from behind the desk and began to walk towards the door. The security guard that had locked the door when he was instructed to, ducked out of the way of the robber. "Unlock it." The robber pointed at the door with his weapon. Eddy jumped up. He saw his chance. He was going to tackle him from behind.

"Don't!" The security guard spoke up. The robber spun around to face Eddy with his gun pointed at him.

"Don't be a hero, you old fool!" He tightened his grip on the gun.

Eddy raised his hands to show submission. The robber turned and fled out of the bank without ever firing a single shot. Eddy was relieved that no one had been hurt, but annoyed that the man had escaped. He felt that familiar adrenaline rush that had assaulted him anytime he had chased after a suspect.

"Why did you do that?" Eddy demanded as he ran past the guard. The guard appeared to be in shock. He was armed, but didn't even attempt to go after the robber. Eddy shook his head and ran out onto the sidewalk. He no longer felt the stiffness in his knee or the exhaustion from waiting in line. His adrenaline was pumping. But the moment he stepped outside, he heard the screech of tires. A car sped off down the street. Eddy couldn't even catch the license plate as it took off too fast.

"Gone," he mumbled. He reached for his radio to call in the robbery, only to be reminded once again that he no longer wore a radio, that he was no longer an active police officer. He heard screeching sirens in the distance that alerted him to the fact that someone had called the police. He felt miserable as he stepped back inside the bank. The pretty brunette offered the little boy an assortment of lollipops. He shook his head and clung to his father. Eddy scowled in the direction of the security guard who talked with the bank manager. He was tempted to leave before the police arrived, but he knew that every witness mattered.

There was a smattering of conversation between the other people at the bank. Eddy realized that he must have had a foul expression on his face because not a single one of them approached him. He looked over at the teller. She stared at the door as if she was looking for someone or something. Her hands were clenched together so tightly that he could see the skin on her knuckles turning white. Eddy started to walk over to her, but before he could reach her, the doors of the bank burst open.

The entire lobby flooded with police officers. Eddy raised his hands cautiously. One of the officers approached him with a stern look in his eyes.

The officer eyed Eddy for a moment, then broke into a wide smile.

Eddy was a little surprised by his reaction until he saw a familiar face walk through the door. Detective Brunner, a young detective that he knew from a previous case he had gotten mixed up in and who he had occasionally given advice to.

"Eddy, can't say that I'm surprised to find you here."

"What do you mean by that?" Eddy frowned.

"I mean that this is the first bank robbery in this town in over ten years, and you are a witness." Detective Brunner shook his head. "It just seems fitting to me I suppose."

Eddy sighed with remorse. "A lot of good it did for me to be here."

"I'm sure that you had a clear grasp of the situation and the risks involved. It says a lot to me that everyone survived, Eddy. Too many times people play cowboy when there are lives at risk."

"I guess you're right." Eddy wasn't convinced. He felt ancient as the young cops milled about taking statements from the witnesses. He guessed that each one judged him for the fact that he did not handle the situation or at least stop the robber from escaping.

"Wait here for me," Detective Brunner

instructed. "I'll be back to get your statement shortly."

"Sure," Eddy agreed even though what he really wanted to do was get out of there. Eddy watched as Detective Brunner went to speak to one of the officers. Eddy felt like he was in a bit of a daze as he watched him. He was still trying to process what had just happened. Eddy noticed the teller talking to a police officer. She was still shaking.

"Sorry about the wait, Eddy," Detective Brunner apologized. "Can you tell me what happened?" He asked as he pulled out his notepad and pen.

"To be honest I was standing in line for some time before I even realized that a crime was taking place. This guy was clever."

"And how did you notice what happened?"

"Well, usually there are more tellers at the counter. That was the first thing that made me feel like something wasn't right. I looked towards the office, to see if the manager noticed the line. I saw the other tellers in there with the manager and another man. I noticed that the other man had a gun in his hand. Then he revealed himself."

"The security guard said you went after the suspect." Detective Brunner looked him in the eyes. "That was risky."

"I didn't catch him, I'm not even sure what I would have done if I did. He disappeared around the corner then sped off in a car. I didn't even get the plate." Eddy shook his head. "I guess I'm not as quick as I used to be."

"Do you remember any details about the suspect? Could you give a description to a sketch artist?" Detective Brunner looked hopeful.

"No, I'm sorry. He had a cap and dark glasses on, I couldn't really see his face. He was white, stocky, probably about six feet tall, brown hair."

"That's good. That's a good start." Brunner nodded. Eddy suspected that he was trying to make him feel better. He had given the detective absolutely no evidence to work with.

"Have you ever seen a case like this before? I mean if I hadn't seen the gun I wouldn't even have known the bank was being robbed," Eddy said.

"Actually, it was only after the manager refused to unlock the vault that the suspect started threatening the hostages. I think if the manager had complied, the suspect might have left without the customers ever knowing," Detective Brunner explained.

"That would have been an interesting robbery." Eddy couldn't stop thinking about whether he could have done more to stop the robbery. "I hope that you're able to catch him."

"We're going to do our best to do just that. Just lay low for a while, Eddy. Whoever did this is still on the loose, and I'd hate for you to be in any danger."

"Don't worry about that, Detective, I can handle myself."

"I'm sure you can, Eddy. I'm sure you can." Detective Brunner gave him a light pat on the back. Eddy tried not to take that as an insult.

Although Detective Brunner's words were kind, Eddy doubted that he was really taking him seriously. The problem with young detectives was they didn't remember a time when their elders knew better. Eddy was raised in a generation that revered their elders, while Brunner had grown up in a time when many things that the previous generation did was questioned.

"If you need my help just let me know." Eddy met his eyes.

"Okay, sure." Detective Brunner's smile appeared staged.

Chapter Two

Eddy left the bank with a headache. He still didn't have the cash out that he needed for Samantha's birthday, and now he had the robbery on his mind. He wasn't sure that he was going to be able to make it to the party that was planned for that evening. He had waited until the last minute as usual. He decided he would just use his credit card, something that he hated to do. He preferred the feel of real money in his hands. Credit cards seemed like an invitation for someone to rob him, both the banks by charging interest, and the hackers that could steal all of his information.

The real problem was that he had no idea what to get Samantha for her birthday. He wanted something to show how much he valued her, but he didn't want it to be too mushy or give her the wrong idea. Buying a gift for a guy friend was simple, but buying a gift for a female friend seemed impossibly complicated. He decided that he needed some reinforcements. He paused beside his car and pulled out his cell phone. As he dialed Walt's number he watched the rest of the witnesses being released from the bank. He could see their shaken expressions. It hadn't been the most pleasant experience for Eddy either, but he was used to a little bit of danger.

"Hi, this is Walt, leave a message."

Eddy rolled his eyes. He knew exactly what Walt was doing. He was sitting on his back porch having his lunch. Walt was very particular about how he did things, and always stuck to the same daily schedule. Eddy guessed that answering the phone during a meal was not on the schedule. He hung up the phone and climbed into his car. He noticed through the side window that the security guard was walking down the sidewalk. Eddy watched him for a minute. As Eddy watched, the teller that he usually saw at the bank ran after the security guard. She caught up with him at the corner. Eddy continued to observe until the ring of his cell phone grabbed his attention. He looked down at the caller ID to see that it was Walt. When he looked back up the pair that had been standing at the corner were gone.

"Hello?"

"Hi Eddy, it's Walt. Did you call me?"

"Yes, I did." Eddy could barely focus on the conversation. He searched the sidewalk and the crosswalk for the teller and the security guard. He didn't see any sign of them. "Oh yes, I did. I was hoping that you could meet me in town and help me find something for Samantha's birthday."

"You still haven't bought her anything?" Walt's tone was reproachful. "Eddy, I offered to go with you last week."

"I know, I know. So, can you help me or not?"

"Sure, I can be there in about twenty minutes. Where do you want to meet?"

"I guess at Forrest, there's a couple of shops there."

"I'll be there."

After Eddy hung up the phone he swept his

gaze over his surroundings once more. He hoped to spot the teller or the security guard. Instead, all he saw were people milling about to get a look at the bank which had been roped off with police tape. Eddy sighed and started the car. He tried to push the bank robbery out of his mind. He needed to get himself to focus on a present for Samantha. He had no idea what to get her. She was too smart to just get her any old gift. He knew that she would think about why he had bought her what he bought her, which meant that he had to think about it, too.

As he drove to Forrest, he noticed that there were quite a few people walking around. He found himself checking each face to see if it was the security guard or the teller. When he reached Forrest he parked his car along the street beside a deli. He could grab a sandwich while he waited for Walt to show up. The deli was one of his favorite places to eat. It was run by an older Hungarian woman whose accent was so thick that Eddy couldn't understand a word she said. But it didn't matter because the food was delicious and her smile was always warm. When he stepped inside she wasn't smiling. She spoke in a fast and emotional tone to the man beside her. Eddy recognized him as her husband who often did deliveries for the deli.

Eddy paused beside the counter. He wished he understood enough of their language to know what had happened to make her so upset.

"Is everything okay?" Eddy met her eye when she finally turned to look at him.

"It's fine." She cleared her throat. "Usual?"

Eddy nodded. He looked at her with sympathy. As her husband stepped out from behind the counter, Eddy offered his hand to him in greeting. He was a quiet man who Eddy rarely heard speak. He took Eddy's hand in a firm shake.

"Is there anything I can do to help?"

"She's just upset about the bank robbery." He spoke in perfect English. Eddy was a little shocked. He had always assumed that the man had the same thick accent as his wife, but once he thought about it he realized that he hadn't ever heard the man speak in English before.

"Oh, you've heard about it?" Eddy frowned.

"Yes, the news spread fast. She is worried that we will be hit next."

"Tell her not to worry. Bank robbers go for big jobs, not little places. Okay?" Eddy smiled.

"Oh? You know this for sure?" The man narrowed his eyes.

"Well, just from experience. I am a retired police officer."

"I will tell her, thank you." He seemed relieved as he stepped behind the counter to tell his wife. Eddy ordered his sandwich, but it was hard for him to enjoy it. As he ate it he was fuming. He thought of all of the other small businesses on the street that would be impacted by the robbery. The ripple effect that crime had on a town always bothered him. When he finished his sandwich he gave a final few words of reassurance to the owners before stepping out of the deli.

"Eddy, there you are."

Eddy nearly bumped into Walt as he stepped out onto the sidewalk. "Oh, I didn't think that you'd be here yet."

"Just arrived. I was going to call your phone, but here you are. Are you all right? You look a little pale."

"I'm fine." Eddy nodded. "I'll feel better once I have something picked out for Samantha."

"That's why I told you to start early. There's no better feeling than being prepared."

Eddy grimaced and nodded. He was not in the mood for one of Walt's lectures, but he knew that his friend only had good intentions.

"I just can't figure out what she would like."

"Samantha is a tough one when it comes to gifts. Let's just take a walk along the shops and see what catches our attention." Walt gestured to the first store in a long line of small shops. Eddy nodded again. He was not much of a shopper, but he was relieved to have some help. As Eddy and Walt made their way through the shops Eddy did his best not to mention the robbery. He wanted some time to sort it out in his head before he brought anyone else into the situation. His mind kept playing back the scene, which made it difficult to focus on frilly coffee mug cozies and plaques with cute sayings carved on them.

"Eddy, you haven't pointed out anything," Walt said. "If you don't come up with something soon I'm going to think that your heart isn't really in this."

"It's just a gift, Walt." Eddy sighed. "Maybe I should just get her a gift card."

"Nope sorry, that's not going to fly with Samantha."

Eddy wondered for a moment if he even wanted to go to the birthday party anymore. Then he remembered that it was for Samantha. She had become a very good friend of his, and he didn't want to hurt her by not being part of her celebration. He caught sight of something shimmering on a display nearby.

"Walt, what do you think?" Eddy pointed to the necklace in the display.

"It's nice I guess." Walt grimaced.

"What?" Eddy glanced over at him.

"Well, you know, buying a woman jewelry."

"Huh?"

"I mean, that's a big step." Walt cleared his throat.

"Step?" Eddy squinted at him. "It's just a birthday gift."

"To you, and to me, it's just a birthday gift."

Eddy stared at the necklace.

"Would you like to see it out?" The clerk behind the counter smiled at him.

"No, I better not." Eddy shook his head. "I just don't know what to get her. Flowers?"

"Eh." Walt frowned. "I never understood giving flowers as a gift. They're going to die, you know? It's only a matter of time before their bright, perfect petals shrivel and fall."

"Then what am I supposed to get her?" Eddy sighed with frustration.

"Hey, I just got her a card. You're the one hung up on getting her a gift. Keep it simple. A card, a signature, and everybody is happy."

"I know that. But Samantha's always so caring towards us and I just want to do something to brighten up her day." Eddy offered an awkward smile. "It's a little out of the norm for me."

"I can see that." Walt chuckled. "All right, let's figure it out. No jewelry, no flowers, don't ever buy a woman clothes, trust me. I know!" He snapped his fingers. "A book!"

"A book?" Eddy narrowed his eyes. "Are you sure about that?"

"I'm sure. Samantha's always looking for something new to read. I think that would be a great gift."

"All right." Eddy nodded. "I think that's a good idea. I'll check out the bookstore on the way home."

***

Eddy stepped into the bookstore with some hesitation. He still had no idea what to buy for Samantha, but he knew he was running out of time. It didn't help that the shelves of the bookstore were covered by hundreds of books. All of the different sections began to blur together. He was about to ask for help from the young woman at the counter when one section caught his attention.

"True crime. Perfect."

As a retired crime journalist he was sure that Samantha would enjoy a good book about an actual crime. However, he had to figure out which one she might not have.

"Are any of these new releases?" He turned towards the woman at the desk.

"First shelf, top row." She smiled, but it was a forced expression. Eddy sensed that she was a shy person. He began looking over the titles available.

Many were gorier than he would choose for Samantha. She was a strong and intelligent woman, but he didn't want the stories to be too violent. He noticed a book at the very end of the row. It was slimmer than the others.

"Unsolved Bank Heists." He read the title out loud. When his fingertips touched the book, he felt a faint shiver race along his spine.

"That seems fitting for today." The woman behind the desk had walked over to him in time to hear his words. "There was just a robbery at the local bank."

"Hm. Maybe a little too real?" He raised an eyebrow.

"I like the ones that aren't solved yet." She smiled again, and this time it was more natural. "True crime is fun to read, but I like books like these that are the real mysteries. It's kind of exhilarating to think that you might be able to figure something out that the police didn't."

Eddy smiled. "It's perfect." He knew that Samantha would adore an opportunity to investigate any crime. After he paid for the book he walked back to his car. As he walked he thought about the robbery. What bothered him most about it was that the robber had been so bold. Most wouldn't be as daring as he had been. They would be worried about whether they were going to be caught. This man didn't seem the least bit worried. Eddy shook his head and reminded himself that he had a birthday party to attend.

Chapter Three

Eddy adjusted his tie. He never quite understood why men were expected to wear them. They are uncomfortable, they didn't cover anything, or accentuate anything, they were just an annoying extra piece of material that always managed to get out of place. But he still wore them on special occasions. He thought it was impolite not to. Samantha's party was a special occasion. He straightened his shoulders and prepared to knock on the door. Despite the fact that Samantha had invited him over several times it felt as if this was his first formal visit. He wondered if he should have brought wine along with his present. He felt as if he was showing up empty handed. He raised his hand to knock just as someone walked up behind him.

"Don't you look snazzy."

There was no mistaking that voice, or that attitude. Eddy turned around and smiled.

"Hello Jo. You look lovely this evening."

He was only attempting to be polite, but the truth was Jo could look lovely in a bed sheet. With her long, thick, black hair and her lithe figure she filled out any dress nicely. The one she wore that evening was much more slinky than usual. It split at the knee of her right leg.

"Thanks. Are you going in?" She looked towards the door. Eddy's hand still hovered over it. Eddy realized how ridiculous he must look. He gave a solid knock on the door and then took a step back.

"I heard about what happened." Jo reached out and lightly touched Eddy's elbow. "You were there, weren't you?"

Eddy stared at her for a long moment. He had no idea how she could know that. He hadn't told Walt, or anyone else that he had been at the bank.

"I'm fine. I'd rather not talk about it." He tilted his head towards the door. "Don't want to ruin the party."

"Sure." Jo nodded. "I'll keep it to myself."

Eddy smiled at her as the door swung open. Samantha beamed at both of them.

"Hi! Thanks for coming!"

"Happy birthday!" Jo gave Samantha a quick hug before she stepped inside. Eddy held his gift bag out in front of him as if it were a shield of some kind.

"Happy birthday, Samantha."

"Oh Eddy, you didn't have to get me a gift." She took the bag from him. "Come in, the food has just arrived."

Eddy moved past her into the villa. He spotted Walt already seated at the table. He appeared to be evaluating the assortment of Chinese food that was spread across the dining room table.

"Smells delicious." Eddy sat down beside Walt.

"Hmm, as long as it doesn't have MSG." Walt continued to study the meals.

"The sign said no MSG," Samantha said as she

and Jo joined them at the table.

"Right, well anyone can make a sign."

"If you don't want it, I'll eat it, Walt." Eddy grinned. "I'm starving."

"Well, let's eat then." Samantha distributed chopsticks. "There's forks in the kitchen if you need them." Eddy plowed right into his honey chicken, one of his favorite dishes.

"So Sam, have you made any birthday resolutions?" Jo skewered a piece of pork with one of her chopsticks.

"Oh boy, am I supposed to do that?" Samantha laughed. "Actually, I have made one. I'm going to go back to work."

"But I thought you were retired?" Eddy looked across the table at her.

"I am retired, but I miss it. I love writing and I don't see anything wrong with doing a little moonlighting, even if it's just for fun."

"Only you would think crime journalism could be fun," Walt said with disbelief.

"Well, then I guess my birthday gift will be perfect for you." Eddy's voice rose with pride.

"Oh?" Samantha stood up. "I can't wait any longer, I'm going to have to open it."

"Well, I didn't exactly wrap it, it's just in a bag." Eddy laughed.

Samantha reached into the bag and pulled out the book. "Oh wow, Eddy, this is great! Now, you all have to leave so I can start reading." She winked at them.

"Well, those aren't the only unsolved bank heists," Jo piped up. She winced when Eddy shot a look in her direction. It was too late. Samantha seized on the topic.

"Did you hear about that awful robbery?" Samantha clucked her tongue. "I can't believe it happened right in town. Did you hear anything from your police contacts about it, Eddy?"

Eddy smiled a little. "I might know a thing or two about what happened."

"Well, then you should fill us in." Walt leaned

34

forward with a pained look on his face. "How much did they take?" Being a retired accountant Walt's mind was always focused on the numbers.

"I heard it was about five hundred thousand. Give or take." Eddy shrugged.

"That's not a bad haul for a small bank." All eyes shifted to Jo in reaction to her comment. "I'm just saying it was a lot to rake in." Jo rolled her eyes. "It's not like I'm admiring the crime."

"It was a lot." Eddy grew thoughtful. It was likely more than the bank would normally have on hand. Maybe the robber knew that there would be a surplus of funds available. It seemed like too much of a coincidence to think that he just got lucky, but maybe he did.

"Do they have a description of the robber?" Samantha asked. She sat back down at the table and put her book down beside her.

"He was white, mid-thirties, stocky and tall. Left-handed, definitely left-handed." Eddy nodded.

"Wow, that's a pretty good description. Now facial features?" Samantha pressed.

"He was wearing a cap and big sunglasses. I couldn't really see his face."

Everyone grew silent at the table. Eddy didn't realize his mistake until Jo nudged his foot under the table.

"You were there?" Samantha's eyes widened with horror. "In the bank when it was robbed?"

"Well, I might have been standing in line." Eddy shrugged. "I mean, it's not a big deal."

"No, you were just a bystander in the middle of a bank robbery. How could you not tell me?" Samantha looked annoyed as she crossed her arms.

"It's not like you didn't already know about it." Eddy frowned. He prepared himself for an interrogation. Samantha was never easily satisfied when it came to a crime.

"I knew it happened, I didn't know you were there, so don't try to twist things around, Eddy.

We're you're friends, you shouldn't be afraid to tell us the truth," she said sternly.

"I wasn't afraid, I just didn't think it was party conversation."

"You still should have told us." Samantha frowned. "You weren't hurt?"

"No, I wasn't hurt." Eddy stared down at the table.

"So, what happened?" Samantha's tone was calmer.

"What happened? I stood in line at a bank that was being robbed and the robber got away."

"You let him get away?" Jo's eyes widened with surprise.

"Jo!" Walt shot her a look. "He's a retired detective not a superhero."

"I didn't mean it that way, I just mean, with Eddy's temper…"

"I don't have a temper," Eddy barked. His heart raced. He felt cornered by the conversation. The anger in his voice created an awkward tension at the table. "I'm sorry." He looked around at his friends. "Look, I didn't tell anyone because I was embarrassed."

"Embarrassed about what?" Samantha raised an eyebrow.

"I tried to stop him, but he got away. I was right there, I could have tackled him, and he got away."

"Eddy, I didn't mean what I said that way." Jo frowned. "I'm sorry. I'm sure there was nothing that you could have done."

"There were hostages." Walt shook his head. "If you had done anything rash someone could have ended up dead."

"Maybe. Or maybe I could have stopped him." Eddy sighed and picked up his drink. "I thought he wouldn't be able to get out the door, but the security guard unlocked it for him. I chased him, but I wasn't fast enough. Sometimes I hate this old body."

"You're not old," Samantha said with

conviction. "Just because we're not in our twenties, that doesn't make us or our bodies old, we are only as old as we feel. You were brave enough to go after the robber, that takes the heart of an alert man."

"Well, I might have the heart of an alert man, but I have the hips of a ninety year old."

"Don't joke about that." Walt's voice deepened with warning. "A broken hip is the last thing you want."

"He's not going to break his hip!" Samantha sputtered.

"You see, this is why I didn't want to bring it up." Eddy frowned. "Now everyone is upset and it's supposed to be a celebration."

"It's okay." Samantha stood up from the table. "I was just surprised. I'm glad you're all right." She hugged Eddy around the shoulders and placed a light kiss on the top of his hat.

"I'm fine, I'm fine." Eddy adjusted his hat and hoped the shadow of the brim would hide the heat in his cheeks. "I just want to enjoy the party."

"Then that's what we'll do." Samantha nodded. "Welcome to the next year of my fabulous existence on this planet."

As the chatter returned to light conversation Eddy felt some relief. He was sure that Samantha was going to demand to know every detail. Instead, she poured everyone wine and they began discussing their favorite birthday experiences. Eddy relaxed and drank an extra glass of wine. By the time the party was wrapping up he had nearly forgotten about the robbery.

"It's getting late." Walt looked at his watch. He had a very specific routine and did not like to stray from it. "I'm going to head home."

"I should go, too. I need to get up early and water my garden." Jo yawned. "Not enough rain lately."

"I'll walk with you," Walt suggested.

"Great." Jo stood up and gave Samantha a hug. "Happy birthday, and many more to come."

"Thanks Jo." Samantha hugged her back. Walt gave her a peck on the cheek.

"I'll help you clean up." Eddy began to gather the plates. He waved to Walt and Jo as they left.

"It was a nice party." Samantha smiled as she took the plates from Eddy. "I didn't expect it to be so much fun."

"I'm glad you enjoyed it." Eddy turned back to the table to clear the rest of the dishes.

"And I'm looking forward to reading the book that you gave me."

Eddy handed her the last of the dishes. "Are you sure you should be washing those on your birthday?"

"Oh Eddy, that's so sweet of you. I don't mind washing the dishes. I'd love to have some company while I work though."

"I can provide that." Eddy leaned up against the counter. "Do you have a dish towel? I can dry."

"It's so terrible to think of how wrong that robbery could have gone." Samantha handed him a towel. "I mean, we all bank there. I just can't imagine what I would have done if I had been there."

Eddy looked over at her and raised an eyebrow. "I didn't do much you know."

"You were there!" Samantha nearly splashed him with bubbles as she enthusiastically scrubbed a plate. "You witnessed the crime and..."

"And, I thought I was here to keep you company, not be interrogated." Eddy laughed. Samantha frowned and eased up on the plate.

"I'm not interrogating you, I'm just curious."

Eddy narrowed his eyes. He had spent so much time figuring out what to get Samantha for her birthday, and all along it had been right under his nose.

"You want to investigate it, don't you?"

Samantha tried to hide a smile by tilting her head away from him. He still saw the corners of her lips perking up.

"Are you going to help me?"

"Well, it is your birthday."

"Great!" Samantha tossed the washcloth into the soapy water. This time she did splash Eddy.

"Watch it!" Eddy drew back from the counter.

"Oops sorry!" Samantha grabbed the towel he had abandoned and used it to mop up his arm and chest. Eddy stood perfectly still as she dried him off.

"Oh, it's all right." He cleared his throat.

"So, tell me everything." She looked at him with hunger in her eyes.

Eddy gestured to the table. "Can we sit?"

Once they were seated Eddy filled Samantha in on every detail of the crime he could remember.

"So far they haven't identified him."

"No fingerprints?" Samantha frowned.

"He was wearing gloves." Eddy shrugged. "It's strange, it was so well planned and the man seemed so relaxed. I've seen robbers before, and they're always tense, sweaty, determined, expecting the worst. This guy, it was almost like he was checking things off on his shopping list."

"Must have been an experienced criminal then," Samantha said. "That might make him easier to identify if he's committed similar crimes in the past."

"Maybe. But would a professional really take such a big risk? I mean, he was letting people come and go out of the bank at first. Anyone, at any time could have noticed what he was up to and alerted the authorities."

"So, when did that change? What made him announce his presence?" Samantha looked at him with interest.

"Detective Brunner told me that the manager of the bank refused to open the vault. He must have known how much money was there. When he did that, the robber made his presence known and threatened lives to get what he wanted."

"So, he had no real interest in violence, but he came prepared for it."

"Seems that way." Eddy nodded. "Just about everything about the robbery was unusual. I would have expected to see it in a bad movie, not in real life."

"That's something that I think everyone hopes that they won't see in real life." Samantha grimaced. "I can say I've never been involved in a situation like that. I don't know how you kept your cool."

"I didn't really." Eddy sighed. "If I had my wits about me better I might have stopped the whole thing."

"You must have left your superhero cape at home." Samantha looked at him with a teasing smile. "You weren't in control, Eddy. It wasn't your fault."

"I know, I know. It's just hard to think of those poor people. They were so scared."

"Weren't you, Eddy?" Samantha met his eyes.

"I guess I was a little. It was just so unexpected." He shook his head. "There were very few times that I stumbled upon a crime in progress. Usually I knew what I was walking into."

"It must have been pretty disturbing when you realized what was happening."

"It was." Eddy nodded. "I just hope he gets caught."

"I think if we work together on it he won't have a chance of getting away." Samantha smiled.

"I don't doubt that for a second, Sam." He chuckled.

Chapter Four

Eddy hung his hat on the rack beside his front door. He waited for a moment to be sure that it was settled correctly on the hook. There were very few things he valued in life, but his hat was one of them. It felt like it was a part of him. He turned the lock on the door and took a deep breath. It had been a long and strange day. It wasn't until he was alone again that he realized he was a little spooked. He had witnessed a crime, and the robber had seen him as well. He was sure that the robber was not the least bit concerned about him, nor would he bother to hunt down his address, but Eddy checked all of the windows in his villa just the same.

When he went to bed his mind was still cluttered with all of the small details of the crime. It bothered him that he couldn't piece them together in a way that made sense. It felt as if he had just fallen asleep when his cell phone began to ring. He fumbled for it on his nightstand. When he opened his eyes he saw sunlight filtering in through his window. He didn't think it was possible that he had slept all night, but apparently he had. He managed to grab hold of his phone then looked at the caller ID.

When he saw who it was he answered right away.

"Good mor- I mean hello, I mean-" He coughed to try to loosen up his voice.

"I'm sorry, did I wake you?" Detective Brunner's voice sounded rushed.

"It's okay, I must have overslept. What's going on?"

"Could you meet me for breakfast?"

"Sure. Is it about the case?"

"Yes. At 'Pancakes on Main' around eight."

"I'll be there."

Eddy hung up the phone and groaned. He had no interest in rushing out of bed, but his interest in the case was enough to drive him to his feet. He stumbled through getting dressed and didn't even flip on the television for the morning news before heading out the door.

When Eddy arrived at the restaurant it was pretty busy. It was early enough for the before work crowd and the truck drivers to be getting their breakfast. He spotted Detective Brunner towards the back of the restaurant. As he made his way over to him he noticed that quite a few of the people he passed were talking about the robbery.

"It's such a relief."

"I'm glad that we can feel safe again. He won't be robbing any other banks, that's for sure."

Eddy thought it was strange for people to be talking that way. He sat down across from Detective Brunner who looked up at him with a broad smile.

"I just wanted to let you know that we found the bank robber."

"Oh really? Did you catch the guy?" Eddy grinned with anticipation. Detective Brunner waited long enough for Eddy to place his order before he began filling him in.

"In a manner of speaking we caught him. We found him dead in his house," he said. "We're not sure who took him out yet, but we're pretty positive that he is the man who robbed the bank."

"How do you know? Fingerprint ID?" Eddy leaned further across the table. He was completely drawn in as he tried to visualize the scene that Detective Brunner had walked into.

"No, he had some of the cash in his possession. The serial numbers matched the money that had been stolen." Detective Brunner smiled triumphantly.

"Was it all there?" Eddy's eyes narrowed.

"Not all of it, no, but enough. We figure he stashed the rest somewhere. Whoever offed him did us a favor. It looks like I might be able to close the robbery case soon."

"Aren't you going to look into who murdered him?" Eddy picked up his drink, but he didn't take a sip. He wanted to figure out what the detective was thinking.

"Yes, of course." Detective Brunner nodded. "But I doubt that they'll assign much manpower to it. It can be assumed that he was engaged in the criminal element, and that criminal element caused his death."

"Wow." Eddy raised an eyebrow. "That doesn't sound very committed."

"Are you telling me that you really think we should waste a lot of police resources on investigating this murder? You were there, Eddy. There was a little boy there, do you think he wasn't affected by this?" Detective Brunner shook his head. "I mean I'll do my job, but I'm not going to bend over backwards seeking justice for a person like that."

"Justice doesn't pick and choose, Detective. It is not something that can be bent or altered. It is what it is. Justice is for everyone, even the ones we don't like." He shook his head. "If you start buying into the idea that there are good people and bad people in the world you're going to be driven crazy. At some point you have to realize, no matter how uncomfortable it makes you, that we are just people. As a detective you have an obligation to seek justice for everyone."

"I don't know if I can see things like that." Detective Brunner frowned. "What I see are average citizens going about their day, and a monster that feels he has the right to disrupt all of that."

"Now the monster's dead. So, what kind of monster do you think kills a monster?" Eddy gazed across the table at the detective. Detective Brunner looked a little confused as he studied Eddy.

"Another monster," he said frowning.

"Half right." Eddy took a swig of his drink. "A bigger monster. If that's how you want to see things fine. You don't want to get justice for a monster, what about catching someone who is even worse?"

"I didn't really think about it that way."

"I know you didn't. But you should. Because the more murders this monster gets away with, the bigger he gets. So, that's why it matters, Brunner."

Detective Brunner nodded a little. He set his fork back down on his plate. "Well, the man's name was John Baker. He has a history of breaking and entering, and assault."

"And how did you happen upon this John Baker?" Eddy raised an eyebrow.

"It was a tip called into the tip line. We really didn't have any specific direction we were going in, just sifting through the usual suspects. Someone called in and said they had overheard a man bragging about the heist and that they had seen him flashing a large amount of money. To be honest with you I thought it was just some kid playing a prank. When we found him and the money, it was a surprise."

Eddy nearly choked on his bite of pancake.

"Are you kidding? He was practically gift wrapped."

"I know, lucky huh?" Detective Brunner smiled.

"Lucky, or something else." Eddy shook his head.

"What do you mean?"

"My best guess is a double-cross. If you're sure he was the one to rob the bank. Someone made that call for a reason. Maybe he has a partner that didn't want to share the money and didn't want to be investigated. Maybe there was a getaway driver who called it in or maybe he is the getaway driver." Eddy finished the last bite of his pancake and piled the silverware onto the plate.

"But if that was the case, why would he leave a portion of the money?" Detective Brunner questioned. "Why go to all the trouble of murdering a man, and then leave the money?"

"Why?" Eddy smiled as if the detective was finally catching onto something he had been wondering all along. "Why would anyone murder a man and walk away from the cash?"

Brunner's eyes widened. "To make it obvious that he was the thief and to make us stop looking or look in the wrong direction."

"Exactly. I'm not trying to tell you how to do your job, Detective, but details can be important."

"Sure, or they can muck up the system. I mean it's entirely possible that what you're saying has nothing to do with the crime. My method is to base my actions on the proof I have, not the theory I imagine." He shrugged.

"Well, if that's what you think." Eddy sighed and sat back in his chair. He tried to impart his wisdom, but it fell on deaf ears. Or maybe Brunner just wanted to move on from the case.

"Thanks Eddy, I appreciate the talk." Detective Brunner stood up from the table. "I'll settle up on the way out."

"Thank you." Eddy finished his drink. He sat at the table for a few minutes after Detective Brunner left.

He ran through in his mind all of the details

of the crime that he knew. He visualized walking into the scene and finding the body. It was the tip call that really set Eddy's mind racing. Someone who was bold enough to not only kill a man, but then call the police in to flaunt the crime, was a very cunning person indeed.

***

As Eddy left the restaurant he felt the weight of Detective Brunner's revelation. Now, not only was there a robbery to solve, but a murder as well. From the detective's attitude it was clear that Eddy might be the only one that was interested in looking into it properly. Was the young man who was killed really even involved in the crime or had he just been a victim? If he was not involved in the crime that meant that the police still had zero leads on who the robber might have actually been.

Eddy thought of Samantha and how she would salivate at the news of a double-cross or even a frame job. He smiled to himself at the thought. There was one thing he and Samantha certainly had in common. They both enjoyed a good crime. It was not as if they took pleasure in the crime occurring, it was more that they took pleasure in justice being served. Eddy was so involved in his own thoughts that when he walked through the parking lot he almost walked directly into someone who was approaching from his car.

"Oh, excuse me." Eddy stepped to the side and looked up at the same time. He met the eyes of Owen, a young nurse who worked at Sage Gardens, and one of his closest friends. "Owen, what are you doing here?"

"I came for breakfast, but I'm glad I ran into you." Owen frowned. "I was worried about you."

"Worried about me? Why?" Eddy raised an eyebrow.

"Eddy, I heard what happened at the bank. I saw Detective Brunner leaving. Were you involved somehow?" Owen's features creased with concern. "There are some rumors buzzing around Sage Gardens that you were at the bank at the time of the robbery."

"Wow, I didn't know word was getting around

so fast. Rumors?" He locked his eyes to Owen's. "Spread by whom?"

"One of the residents of Sage Gardens, Paul Carlil, his granddaughter is a teller at the bank. She told her grandfather about it, and she gave him your description. She didn't know your name, but knew you lived at Sage Gardens. I saw him just before and he said he guessed it was you. Was it?"

"Yes, I was there. But I've only told a few people about that. I don't want the whole place to know. You know how the girls can get in a tizzy over those things."

"Sure." Owen nodded, but his concern had not faded. "But are you okay?"

"Yes, I'm okay. Not a scratch on me. A little embarrassed that I didn't stop the guy, but otherwise I'm just fine."

"Are you sure you don't want me to check you out? Stressful situations can wreak havoc on your body," Owen explained. "It'll only take a minute."

"No, I'd rather you didn't. I'm fine. But I appreciate the offer." He smiled. "Just hate to see it happening around here."

"Yes, it's not good for anyone to have that kind of crime in our backyard. Did they catch the robber yet?"

"Well, that remains to be seen." Eddy smiled.

"Uh oh, secrets, huh?" He winked at Eddy. "All right, but when you're ready to fill me in just let me know. I'd love to hear about it."

"It won't be long. Just trying to figure out a few details. Then I'll let you know everything there is to know."

"If there's anything I can do to help, just ask." Owen met his eyes. "And try to remember that you're not as young as you used to be."

"Well, Owen, with you around to remind me I don't see how I could forget." Eddy set his jaw.

"I didn't mean it like that." Owen frowned. "I just don't want you to get in over your head with this."

"Don't worry, Owen, I'm not going to hunt down and tackle a bank robber." Eddy chuckled. If he was honest with himself he had thought about it. "I'll be fine."

"All right, I'm going to hold you to that." Owen tilted his head towards the restaurant. "Now, I'm going to have some pancakes."

"They are the best." Eddy watched Owen walk away. He was grateful to have him as a friend. He was about to turn towards his car when a thought occurred to him.

"Owen?" He caught his attention just before he opened the door.

"Yes?" Owen looked back at him.

"You said Paul's granddaughter works at the bank. Do you know her name?"

"Terry, I think."

Eddy smiled. "Thanks."

"No problem. Take it easy, Eddy."

Eddy nodded. As he reached his car, the woman's name stuck in his mind.

Chapter Five

As soon as Eddy returned to Sage Gardens he headed for Samantha's villa. He knew that she would want to be updated on any development in the investigation. When he knocked on the door of her villa, it was not Samantha that opened it.

"Hi Eddy." Jo smiled at him.

"Good morning, Jo. I was looking for Samantha." He looked past Jo and for just a moment wondered if he might have wandered to the wrong villa.

"She's here. We were having coffee." Jo stepped aside to let Eddy in. "She had to take a phone call."

"Oh, I see." Eddy nodded.

"Did you have a good breakfast?" Jo smiled.

"How did you know I had breakfast?" Eddy stared at her.

"You left some syrup behind on your shirt." Jo

laughed.

Eddy looked down to see that there was indeed a trail of syrup on his shirt. "Oops." He frowned.

"Hi Eddy." Samantha stepped in from her bedroom. "Sorry about that, Jo, it was one of my old contacts at the police department."

"Contacts?" Eddy looked over at Samantha.

"Yes, I thought that I would get a head start on the investigation."

"Oh?" Eddy glanced over at Jo. He had expected things to stay just between him and Samantha.

"She clued me in," Jo said. "But don't worry, I'm not getting in the middle of any of this. Samantha might enjoy the hunt, but I'd rather be left to my garden."

"Who did you call? I talked with Detective Brunner this morning."

"Well, then we probably have the same information. I called someone in bookings and he let me know that the case was pretty much solved," Samantha said.

"Well, that was fast." Jo laughed.

"Very fast." Eddy frowned. "Too fast."

"Do you think so?" Samantha looked surprised. "It sounded like it was pretty open and shut to me. The robber was murdered."

Eddy looked from Jo to Samantha and didn't respond. Jo raised her hands in surrender. "I get it, I get it. I was on my way out anyway." She brushed past Eddy as she headed out the door.

"What's that about?" Samantha frowned. "I thought you were over giving Jo the cold shoulder."

"This is already spreading all around Sage Gardens, Samantha. Owen already found out that I was at the bank."

"Eddy, you're going to have to learn to trust people eventually you know."

"Maybe." He smirked a little. "Until then, we're going to have to try to keep this under wraps, because secrecy is going to be our greatest asset."

"What are you talking about?" Samantha looked puzzled. "Now you have me confused. If the case is solved, why the need for secrecy?"

"Because it hasn't been solved. In fact, I think the case just became even more complicated. Not only do we have a robbery to solve, but a murder as well."

"Why do you think that?"

"I think whoever robbed the bank, or at least whoever was behind it, is the one who murdered this man and framed him." Eddy leaned back against the wall. "What I can't figure out is whether the person who was murdered was the man who robbed the bank, or just someone made to look like he robbed the bank."

"Well, if he isn't the robber, then who do you think he was?" Samantha stepped forward, intrigued.

"Maybe an accomplice. Maybe just some poor

sap that the real criminal wanted to take the fall. It's quite possible that the murdered man knew nothing about the robbery at all."

"How can you be sure if that's the case?"

"I can't. At least not without a little more information. I feel like I'm missing something."

"Well, let's see if we can figure it out." Samantha's enthusiasm made Eddy's head spin. He appreciated that she was so interested, but he still couldn't wrap his head around what had happened.

"Not here, let's go down by the water. I need to clear my head."

"Okay." Samantha followed him out the door. Samantha's villa was situated only a few feet from the lake in the center of Sage Gardens. They walked together to a bench beside the water. As Eddy gazed out across the water, Samantha turned to look at him. "So, tell me what is on that brilliant mind of yours?"

"I just need to think a minute." Eddy sat down

on the bench. Samantha sat down as well, and left some room between them. Eddy appreciated the fact that Samantha seemed to intuitively know when he needed a little more space.

Eddy stared out across the pond. Samantha shifted on the bench beside him, but she didn't speak. He felt as if she was giving him time to think. But the more he thought about it, the more he was convinced that something wasn't right.

"Why would the murderer leave the money behind?" He blurted the question out just as a bird lifted out of the tall grass at the edge of the pond. "Unless the victim was being framed for the robbery, no criminal would ever leave some of their profit behind, would they? It just doesn't make sense that you would murder for the money and then leave the money behind."

"It doesn't make sense to me, either. But crimes don't always make sense. Maybe the murderer didn't even know about the bank robbery, or the money. Or maybe after committing the crime there was something that made the killer flee and there was no time to find the money. Or maybe he deliberately left the money. Or maybe it was as simple as the murderer couldn't find the money," Samantha said thoughtfully. "I don't know what other reasons there could be."

"So, you think that it's possible that he was killed for an entirely different reason? By someone who had no idea that he had any money stashed away?" Eddy nodded a little. "I hadn't even considered that."

"It's a stretch. It would be quite a coincidence."

"Maybe we're looking at this from the wrong perspective." Eddy sat back on the bench. "Instead of focusing on what we don't have the information to figure out, what do we have the information to figure out?"

"Well, we know there was a bank robbery." Samantha held up one finger. "That's a fact. One man robbed the bank."

"Wait, wait. We don't know that it was one

man. I only saw one man, but maybe the robber was working with someone who didn't appear to be part of the crime." Eddy snapped his fingers.

"Okay, okay, but before we go off on that tangent let's stick to what we do know. There was a bank robbery, with at least one robber involved."

"Yes. We do know that for a fact. We also know that some of the money from that particular bank robbery was recovered in the home of a man who was murdered. The serial numbers were a match, so there is no question that the money was from the robbery." Eddy knocked his fist against his knee. "So, now that we know that somehow the money from the bank robbery got into this man's home. How are we supposed to figure anything out with that little amount of information?"

"We also know something else." Samantha smiled.

"What?" Eddy frowned. "I thought we listed everything."

"We know that the majority of the money

from the robbery is missing. It was not in the murdered man's house. Which I think can lead us to either presume that whoever robbed the bank had a partner or partners so the money could be split, or they stashed the money somewhere."

"So, someone could still be out there with the rest of the money." Eddy snapped his finger again. "Yes! You're right about that. We're too focused on who the murdered man is. We need to focus on who his partner might be. Where is the rest of the money?"

"Exactly," Samantha said. "Once we figure that out we might be able to get somewhere as far as both the murder and the robbery are concerned."

"Which brings us back to the question of whether there may have been a second robber at the bank. Someone I didn't notice. Maybe even a silent partner." Eddy took a deep breath.

"Do you think that you could recall all of the people that you saw in the bank?" Samantha frowned. "I'm not sure that I could do that."

"I can. I'm sure I can. I just need to focus." He ran his hands across his face and tried to relax.

"Maybe I can help you with that. There were a few times when I was investigating a crime that the person I was interviewing couldn't quite remember a detail that I needed to include in my story. So, I would walk them through some relaxation techniques to help them to remember. Would you like me to try that with you?" Samantha looked at him expectantly.

Eddy didn't want to disappoint her. It sounded like mumbo jumbo to him, but he didn't need to tell her that.

"All right, I'll try it." He nodded. "What do I need to do?"

"It's pretty simple. All you need to do is relax and listen to the sound of my voice." She shifted a little closer to him on the bench. "Make sure that you are comfortable."

"Okay." He did his best to follow her instructions, but it was hard for him to relax with her sitting right next to him. He started to wonder awkward things, like whether he had remembered to put on deodorant when he woke up so quickly that morning, or if she could tell that he hadn't brushed his teeth after his morning coffee. In the middle of all of these jumbled thoughts he heard her voice.

"Just relax, Eddy, take a deep breath and feel all of your muscles begin to relax. Any pain or discomfort that you may be feeling will leave your body. You begin to feel anything out of place in your body or mind, falling right into place. You are comfortable, you are safe, and you can think very clearly."

Eddy was surprised to discover that he was completely immersed in the sound of her voice. It was not difficult for him to follow her directions. He did feel comfortable and safe.

"Now, I'm going to take you to a time when things were very stressful. I want you to remember that you are safe. This is just a memory. You don't have to be afraid, you don't have to be angry. You will see clearly, and your mind will be crisp."

Eddy felt his heart beat quicken some. He didn't like the idea that she would think he was ever afraid of anything. But he knew that was just his ego talking. He drew another deep breath.

"Okay, Eddy, now on the count of three you're going to be back at the bank, waiting in line to complete your transaction. Everything will be fine. You will not be afraid. There is no reason to be worried." Samantha drew her own deep breath then she began to count in a dreamy tone. "One, two, three."

Eddy was jolted into the awareness that he was at the bank. Of course he was still sitting on the bench beside Samantha in front of the lake. But his mind felt as if it had been transported back to the bank at the time the robbery took place.

"Why are you at the bank?"

Eddy tensed a little. He felt a little shy about admitting the reason he was at the bank to Samantha, so he went for a more generic answer. "To take some money out."

"Okay. So you're waiting in line. Are there other people in line?"

"Yes."

"Can you see how many people are waiting?"

Eddy narrowed his eyes. He could see that there were people in front of him, but it was hard to get an exact count. "About five or six."

"Okay. How are you feeling?"

"A little annoyed at the wait."

"Can you see anyone else around the bank? Anyone who is not in line? Maybe someone who is standing alone and watching?" Samantha's voice was still very soothing. She spoke each word with care.

"There is only one teller working. There are some people in the glass office."

"Anyone else? Anyone not waiting in line? Not talking to anyone?" Samantha pressed. Eddy felt some pressure in his memory. He forced himself to pay attention to the people around him instead of the glimmer of the gun. His heart began to pound. His eyes locked on one particular person. Then as if a fast forward button had been pressed, the scene played out at rapid speed. His breath increased slightly. His hands began to tremble. He saw the man in the hat with the gun. But that wasn't where the memory stopped. It stopped when Eddy bolted towards the door, when he realized that the security guard had complied with the robber's request and unlocked the door. His eyes flew open. He felt Samantha's warm hand curl around his shaking fingers.

"Eddy, are you okay?" She squeezed his hand. "You're safe now. It's okay."

"I know I'm safe," Eddy barked. He pulled his hand away from Samantha's. His mind spun as if he couldn't quite figure out where he was. "Did you hypnotize me?" He looked at her with annoyance.

"Maybe." She winced. "Just a little bit."

"Why didn't you tell me that was what you were doing?" Eddy demanded.

"I would have, but I figured that you would

call it mumbo jumbo and refuse to do it." Samantha crossed her arms.

Eddy couldn't exactly argue with that. "Oh well, I might not have said that."

"That's not the point. All that matters was whether it worked. Did it work?" She met his eyes.

Eddy was about to shake his head, then he remembered the last person he had looked at in his memory.

"The security guard." He stood up from the bench in one swift movement.

"The security guard?" Samantha repeated. She stood up as well.

"Yes. I thought it was strange at the time, but I didn't really focus on it. When the robber went to run, the security guard didn't even stop him. He unlocked the door for him. I remember thinking that it was crazy, but I was too busy running after him to really think much about it." His hands balled into fists. "I bet he was in on it. I bet that's why the robber was so relaxed the whole time. In any other robbery the first thing they would have done would have been to subdue the security guard." He gritted his teeth. "I don't know why I didn't think about it before. I bet he was the partner."

"Wait, wait a second, Eddy. If I had been the security guard I might have done the same thing. In fact most security guards are trained to do whatever the robber requests in order to reduce the chance of injury. So, maybe the security guard was just following his training. Or maybe." She placed a hand lightly on Eddy's shoulder. "Maybe he was just scared."

"Maybe." Eddy frowned. "Sure, it's possible that I'm reading too much into it, but he's the only person that I thought of when I thought about who might have been involved."

"I wonder if you noticed anything suspicious about him when you walked into the bank." She studied Eddy intently. "Did he say or do anything that you thought was odd?"

Eddy grimaced. He hadn't thought that far

back. He had thought back to being in line, not back as far as entering the bank. Now that he did, he remembered something.

"Yes, when I walked in, I nodded to him. You know, just as a greeting. He was more concerned with drinking his coffee and he stared straight through me like I wasn't even there. I thought that was a little rude. Also, I had never seen him in the bank before. I just assumed he was new and wasn't taught to be courteous to the customers." He shifted his hat on his head. "But maybe he looked right through me because he was nervous and he didn't want to tip me off to anything."

"Maybe. You might be on to something. A new security guard who acted strangely and then complied with the robber's request so he could escape."

"I'm sure I can get his name from Detective Brunner. Do you think you could work your investigative magic and see if you could get any information on him?" Eddy smiled at her.

"Oh, how charming, Eddy." Samantha

winked. "Yes, if you get me a name I should be able to find some information about him."

"I'll call him now." He pulled out his cell phone. As he waited for Detective Brunner to answer he glanced over at Samantha. She was already scrolling through her contacts on her cell phone. He smiled despite his nature to resist joviality. He might not like the circumstances, but he did enjoy investigating a crime with Samantha. He thought this was going to be a very interesting case as well.

"Hey Eddy, make it quick, I'm in the middle of something."

"Sorry, I just need to know the name of the security guard at the bank."

"What? Why?" He sounded frustrated.

"Just curious about something."

"Eddy listen, I'm trying to get my superior to change his mind and put more manpower into the investigation, but I'm not getting much traction on it."

"Oh, I understand, the brass doesn't want to put too much time into the investigation of the murder of a criminal. But do you know the name of the security guard?"

"What I'm trying to say is you need to stay out of this. I can't have you snooping around, and the aftermath fly back in my face."

"Detective, I'm just asking a simple question about a crime that I was a witness to, that's all." Eddy tried to restrain the annoyance in his voice. He knew that Detective Brunner had a job to do and he was just trying to do it. However, he also knew that a murder had been committed and he might be the only one that cared enough to solve it. Detective Brunner did not seem very interested in finding the truth. Eddy was worried that once someone was branded a criminal not a lot of effort was put into figuring out why they were murdered.

"I can't, Eddy." Detective Brunner hung up the phone before Eddy could respond. Eddy was a bit surprised that he didn't reveal the information as he had been more forthcoming with information in the past.

"Well," Samantha said eagerly.

"He wouldn't give it to me." Eddy grimaced. "But let me try someone else," Eddy said. Samantha nodded hopefully.

Luckily Eddy had another chance at getting the information. That was through Chris. He dialed the number of his contact in the police department crime lab.

"Eddy, it's been a while."

"I know. I'm sorry, I've been a bit busy."

"That's all right, just glad to hear from you. What can I help you with, since I know that you're not calling me to talk sports?"

"Ha, you know me far too well. Actually, I was wondering if you could help me out with a situation."

"A situation, or a case?" The tension in his voice made it clear that he believed it to be the latter.

"Okay, it might be an active case, but I'm not asking for much."

"What is it, Eddy?"

"I need the name of the security guard from the bank robbery yesterday," he said casually.

"Really. Why?" Chris sounded perplexed.

"It's just a hunch I have."

"I don't know, Eddy."

"It's just a name, Chris."

"Okay, let me see if I can get it," Chris said. "Just hold on a minute."

"I appreciate it." Eddy could hear Chris typing in the background.

"It's Karl Connell," Chris said when he came back on the line.

"Thanks."

"You know the drill. You didn't get it from me."

"Of course," Eddy said as he hung up the phone.

He turned back to Samantha. She waited white-knuckled at the edge of the bench.

"His name is Karl Connell. Let's see how long he's been at the bank, and what his life was like before that."

"I'm on it." Samantha smiled and put her phone to her ear. "I'll have to go in so I can have access to my computer as well."

"All right," Eddy complied. "I'll meet you there in a few minutes." He slid his phone back into his pocket and looked out over the water once more as Samantha walked towards her villa. His mind kept returning to the robbery. Had he missed something else? Was there something that could have tipped him off before he noticed the glimmer of the gun? He remembered the teller at the front desk. He also remembered the same teller running after the security guard. An uneasy thought struck him. Could the teller have been involved as well? He hated to even consider it since he had always been rather fond of Terry, but he couldn't rule it out.

As Eddy turned and walked to Samantha's villa he ran through the robbery in his mind again. What about that man who had ignored his attempts to communicate that there was a robbery in progress? Eddy had brushed off his behavior as generational indifference, but now he wondered. When he opened the door to Samantha's villa he overheard her conversation.

"Really? So, no problems at all? Okay, well thank you for your help. If you think of anything, please do let me know." She hung up the phone. Eddy paused just inside the door and looked at her apologetically.

"I didn't mean to interrupt," he murmured.

"You didn't," Samantha said. "But I'm afraid I'm not getting anywhere with Karl, the security guard."

"Oh?" Eddy sat down on the couch. Samantha sat down across from him.

"He has only been employed at the bank for about a month. However, the person I spoke to at the bank only had glowing things to say about him."

"Hm." Eddy frowned.

"Before the bank he worked as a guard at the jail," Samantha explained. "For him to have such a good work history, I wonder if he'd really be willing to break the law."

"Well, money can be a strong influence," Eddy said. "But it does sound unlikely."

"I still have a few rocks I can turn over." Samantha smiled with confidence.

"It's a bit of a dead end, don't you think?" Eddy asked.

"Why?" Samantha looked at him with surprise. "I've never known you to give up on something so quickly."

"I'm not giving up, I just have nowhere to go. If he has such a spotless record at the bank, and in the prison system, I find it hard to believe that he would be involved in the crime."

"Well, we don't know about his record in the prison system yet." Samantha cleared her throat.

"It's not so easy to get information on a prison employee. That's the problem."

"Well, it's not a problem for me." Samantha smiled as she began sliding through her contacts on her phone. "I have plenty of contacts in the prison system from the investigations I've done in the past."

"You would." Eddy did his best not to roll his eyes. He and Samantha didn't always see eye to eye on her past investigations, especially the ones that involved prisoners who claimed to be innocent.

"Do you want me to call or not?" The phone was already at Samantha's ear.

Eddy smiled apologetically. Sometimes his words got ahead of his good sense. Samantha walked away as she chatted on the phone. She was overly protective of her connections and sources. Eddy could respect that to a degree. He'd been stymied more than once in a police investigation because of a journalist refusing to reveal their source. A few minutes later Samantha returned with her phone in her hand and a frown on her face.

"I found out some information, but I'm afraid it might not be very helpful."

"Why not?" Eddy felt disappointed already.

"If we're looking for dirt there isn't any. According to my source at the prison he was a model employee. In fact they were unhappy to lose him when he went into private security," Samantha said. "It looks like we might be barking up the wrong tree here."

"Maybe," Eddy said. "I just can't stop thinking about how he so casually unlocked the door for the robber. Between the two of us we could have stopped him, instead he just let the robber escape."

"Eddy, not everyone is as brave as you." Samantha offered a light smile. "Perhaps he was taking the value of his life into consideration. It wouldn't be unusual for someone to be faced with danger and decide to make the safer choice."

"I guess. I'm still not sure though. He didn't seem frightened to me."

"Some people hide it better than others. He may have been in shock."

"Hm. But he had worked in a prison. It wasn't as if he hadn't been around criminals before. I don't know, I'm just not buying it."

"Well, what we have now is proof that he was a stellar employee while working at the prison. I guess we can keep digging."

"We should get Walt to look into his finances." He snapped his fingers. "If there's something to be found he will find it."

"That's a good idea. But Eddy, we need to be careful." Samantha looked at him with some concern.

"Careful, why?"

"Because if your hunch is wrong and we're not careful, then word could get around about this man's reputation being questioned."

"It's just an investigation."

"Into someone who we don't know did anything criminal. Into someone who relies on his reputation to gain employment," Samantha said sternly. "Even if you suspect someone you still have a responsibility to show courtesy."

"I will don't worry, I won't let anyone know that we are looking into his history. But, he was involved in this, I don't doubt it for a second." Eddy stood up from the couch. "No one is that squeaky clean."

"If your instincts are telling you that then you should follow them. It's not often that I've known you to be wrong, Eddy."

Eddy was a little surprised by her comment. "Thanks Sam."

Chapter Six

On his way to Walt's Eddy noticed Owen stepping into the main office of Sage Gardens. Eddy raised his hand to wave to him, but Owen was already inside. Eddy felt a hint of relief that he didn't have to avoid another attempt from Owen at taking his blood pressure. He was almost at Walt's when he heard someone running up behind him. He stopped and turned to see who it was.

"Owen." Eddy smiled.

"Hey, I thought I spotted you. I just wanted to check in and see how you were doing." He looked at Eddy intently. "You know sometimes reactions to trauma can happen much later than when the actual event took place."

"Owen, I appreciate your concern, but I'm not traumatized."

"I appreciate your opinion, but not many traumatized people know that they're traumatized. It can show up in subtle ways."

"I think that you're overthinking this, Owen. If I felt I was anything but normal, you would be the first one to know. Don't you know that, Owen?" Eddy said. "I'm fine, really."

"Look Eddy, I know that it's hard to be off the police force. I can't even imagine what it will be like when I retire."

"I can tell you this." Eddy looked into his eyes. "When you see someone in need of medical attention, you won't be retired anymore. Just like when I see that justice needs to be done, I'm not going to sit back and do nothing. Either you're going to have to accept that about me or you are going to constantly be worried about me. Trust me, Owen, there are much better ways that you could be spending your time."

"I hear you, I hear you." Owen nodded, but his eyes were still wrinkled with concern. "I just worry about you, Eddy."

"I'm fine." Eddy smiled.

"Good." Owen nodded. "Then I guess I will have to let you get back to work, Detective. You just let me know if there is any way I can help."

"Actually, there might be." Eddy ran a thumb down the curve of his chin as he considered how much to tell Owen.

"Anything." Owen smiled.

"I just need your opinion on something. If someone was to be in a stressful situation, a life or death type of situation…"

"Like the one you were in yesterday?" Owen prompted.

"Yes, just like that one. Do you think that person would be able to remain calm?" he asked with interest.

"Eddy, even if you felt calm, you probably weren't."

"See, that's the problem, Owen, you're thinking like my nurse again. I'm not talking about me. I'm talking about someone else that was there. He was calm, didn't even blink an eye.

No sweat, no flushed cheeks, no nothing. Is that even possible?" Eddy narrowed his eyes.

"Well, it's hard to tell what's going on underneath when you're looking at someone. Sometimes they will appear perfectly calm, but that could only be on the surface. However, there's usually some sign, the tremble of a hand, sweat, widened eyes, something that indicates they are alarmed by the situation."

"This guy wasn't showing any of that," Eddy explained. "When he unlocked the door, he didn't even hesitate."

"I wouldn't say that sounds like someone who was frightened."

"What about in shock? Could someone be that calm if he was in shock?"

"Well, if he was in shock, he wouldn't likely react to direction, or at the very least there would be a delay." Owen looked thoughtful. "But people do react differently to situations. I can tell you what the average person would do, but that doesn't mean that everyone will fall into those parameters. I'm sorry, I wish that I could help you more."

"You have helped." Eddy held out his hand for a handshake. "Thank you, Owen."

Owen gave his hand a firm shake. "Anytime, Eddy. You know where I am if you need me."

Owen turned and walked back towards the main office. Eddy turned back to Walt's villa. He was more determined than ever to find out the truth about Karl Connell.

***

Eddy knocked on the door of Walt's villa. Walt opened it after Eddy's knuckles hit the wood a third time.

"Eddy." Walt smiled. "How did I know that I'd be seeing you?"

"I don't know." Eddy lifted an eyebrow. "How did you know?"

"Maybe a little bird called me?" Walt opened the door further for Eddy.

"A little bird named Samantha?" Eddy

stepped inside.

"Maybe so."

"Well, I am here for some help, Walt."

"Sure. Do you need a muffin recipe? Stuck on a crossword?" Walt folded his arms over his chest. "I'll be glad to help."

"Not that kind of help." Eddy laughed. "I need you to see if you can find out about someone's finances for me."

"Ah, there's the truth I've been waiting for," Walt said. "I'm not going to do it."

"Walt. Think of the community. I need you to look into a potentially dangerous man, for the sake of our community." He met Walt's eyes. "Someone has to do it. You don't have to dig too deep just see what you can find out."

"So, it's the bank robber then?" Walt frowned.

"No. I suspect he is an accomplice. So far Samantha and I haven't been able to turn up anything criminal in his past."

"What's the name?"

Walt walked over to his computer.

"Karl Connell. He's the security guard at the bank," Eddy said. Walt's eyes widened.

"What makes you think he's involved?" Walt typed away on his keyboard.

"Just a hunch of mine." Eddy leaned over the back of Walt's chair and peered at the computer screen. Walt stopped typing. He spun his chair around, which nearly knocked Eddy off balance.

"I'm sorry, Eddy, I don't know if you think I have a magic wand or something. What do you expect me to find?"

"I don't know, but you've managed to find things before." Eddy stared hard at him.

"For murder suspects, Eddy, for people we were certain were bad guys. This man is a bank security guard. I have done it before, but now you're asking me to do something just because of a hunch. I do trust your instincts, Eddy, but you were there at the time of the crime. Your adrenaline was pumping, too."

"What are you trying to say?"

"I'm trying to say that maybe you're remembering things a little differently because there was so much going on. You had your mind focused on the robber, not on the security guard. So, you say that he was too casual about letting the robber out, but that could have been how it looked through the chaos in your mind."

"There was no chaos in my mind." Eddy turned away from Walt for a moment. He took a breath deep enough to make his shoulders rise and fall. When he turned back Walt eyed him warily.

"I'm not accusing you of anything, Eddy. I'm just saying that we need to be cautious."

"Of course." Eddy nodded. "Just see what you can find."

"Okay," Walt agreed.

"I was also thinking that if I can get you copies of his telephone records would you see if you can work out if he has made contact with anyone suss recently."

"Oh." A grimace flickered across Walt's features. He thought about it for a moment. Then he nodded. "I guess I could do that. But how would you get the information?"

"You just let me worry about that."

Eddy walked out of Walt's villa with blood pounding through his veins. He felt like he was getting questioned and blocked at every turn. He knew without question that Karl was involved somehow, but getting anyone else to agree with him was like pulling teeth. He couldn't blame Samantha or Walt, the man had an impeccable record. It didn't make sense that he would throw all of that away to be involved in a bank robbery. Eddy knew there was only one way that he was going to get the information that he needed. He needed to call Chris again. He walked back towards his villa. He was just about to step inside when his cell phone began ringing. He pulled it out to see that it was Samantha.

"Hello?"

"Hey Eddy, I just wanted to see how things were coming along. Did you find out any more information about Karl?"

Eddy sighed. "Not yet. I'm trying to get some more information on him right now."

"Okay, well why don't you meet me in an hour and we can go over anything new we've discovered?"

"Sounds good," Eddy agreed. He was in a hurry and trying to rush her off the phone, without being rude. He hung up the phone with Samantha and immediately dialed Chris' number.

"Eddy." Chris answered on the first ring.

"Hi, Chris. I need another favor, please," Eddy said getting straight to the point.

"What is it, Eddy?"

"All I need are the telephone records for Karl Connell's phone, the security guard that was at the bank robbery yesterday."

"Wait what? You mean his witness statement?"

"No, I mean his telephone records. I know that you can get into them."

"Not legally I can't. Not without a search warrant."

"Now now, Chris, if I had a search warrant, would I be calling you?"

"You couldn't have a search warrant, you're not an active police officer."

"Exactly. All I need from you are the telephone records."

"What? That's it?" He chuckled. "Well, let me get that right to you. Would you also like my job? Or perhaps my house?"

Eddy rolled his eyes. "Let's not be dramatic."

"Oh, I'm not. I'm telling you right now that getting you that information is not easy."

"So, when can I expect it?" Eddy braced himself. There was a long silence on the other end of the line.

"A couple of hours." The line disconnected and Eddy smiled. He knew he wouldn't get nearly as far without his acquaintances in the police department. He also knew what a risk it really was for his friend to help him out. Eddy hated to ask so much of him, but he knew that he was one of his best contacts. There was very little that Chris couldn't find out for him, and despite the fact that Chris took his orders from the police chief he always wanted to please Eddy. It might have had something to do with the fact that Eddy had taught him so much when he was first hired. No matter what the reason was their friendship had remained strong over the years.

***

Within a few hours Chris proved that he had come through, yet again. Eddy's phone buzzed with a notification that he had a new message. He checked it to find that it was from Chris.

I've dropped it in your mailbox.

Eddy quickly walked out of his villa and down the path to his mailbox. He looked around to make sure no one was watching him and quickly unlocked it. As expected, inside was an envelope.

He walked back to his villa and opened the envelope. Eddy shook his head with admiration as he pulled out the phone records. He tried not to think about the type of risk Chris was taking for him. He knew that Chris shared Eddy's desire for justice that didn't always follow the rules and regulations that police had to follow.

As Eddy glanced over the records all he saw was a bunch of numbers. He knew that Walt would be able to quickly work out if there was a pattern, a certain number that was called often or around the time of the robbery. However, it was late and his friend went to bed at the exact same time each night. Eddy set the papers on his desk and stood up to stretch. He walked towards the living room where the television entertained empty space. He stared for a moment at the images that flickered across the screen. As he focused on the show there was a knock at the door. He looked up towards it. A quick glance at his watch informed him that it was after nine o'clock, rather late for any visitors. He walked over to the door and opened it.

"Samantha, what are you doing here?"

Samantha looked at him with narrowed eyes. "What do you mean what am I doing here? You were supposed to meet me to talk about the case."

"Oh right!" Eddy grimaced and stepped back from the door. "You can come in if you like."

Samantha stepped inside, but she did not smile. Since she was normally such a cheerful person, Eddy noticed that she did not offer him her usual greeting.

"Is everything okay?"

"I just don't want to be left out of the loop," Samantha pleaded. "It might not seem important to you, but I really want to get to the bottom of this crime. It's important to me that our neighborhood bank is a safe place to go."

"Well, the robber is dead." Eddy shrugged. "I don't think he'll be a repeat offender."

"Very funny." Samantha smirked. "But what I'm saying is that if there is another person involved, they might very well try again. Once a town becomes an easy target it can turn into a crime spree."

"Samantha, I think you're worrying just a little too much." Eddy gestured to the couch. "Sit with me and I'll update you on everything that is going on."

"Sure." Samantha plonked herself down on the couch. She picked up the remote and turned off the television that Eddy had been using as background noise. Eddy sat down beside her.

"I spoke to Walt about whether he could look into the guard's financials. He said he would see what he can find out, but he wasn't really willing to dig too deep. He also said that he would look into his phone records, but only if I could provide him with the information. So, I reached out to my contact in the police department and was able to get copies of the phone records."

"Oh, that's great!" Samantha smiled then, finally. "Let's take them over to Walt."

"No, we can't do that, look at the time." Eddy

pointed to his watch. Samantha's eyes widened.

"Oh, yes you're right. Walt is a creature of habit. I'm sorry, I didn't realize it was so late."

"Hey, I'm the one who didn't show up for our meeting." Eddy smiled at her. "I'm glad you came by. I'm sorry that I forgot."

"It's okay. I've been thinking about what you said about the security guard and how you suspect he might be involved. It occurred to me that if Karl had a spotless record in the prison system, what would drive him to change jobs? The benefits and pay are much higher in the prison system. I thought maybe the bank offered something better so I looked into it. Comparing everything from health insurance to paid vacation, Karl had a much better deal as a prison guard." She shook her head. "I think you're right, something does not add up here."

"It is possible the stress of working in the prison every day got to him. I've known guys that happened to. Working in a prison is like living in another world. It can feel like you're in prison as well. Maybe he just got burnt out?" Eddy shrugged. "I don't think that's the case, but it's something to consider."

"You're absolutely right. I considered that. Then I considered what else could have happened and I remembered an article I wrote years ago about a murderer and prison guard getting married when the murderer was released. They had fallen in love. It made me wonder if perhaps Karl had gotten too close to one of the inmates. Not necessarily romantically."

Eddy's eyes widened. "Oh wow. I hadn't even thought about that. You mean, what if he became friendly with one of the inmates? Maybe they taught him the ins and outs of the robbery or hooked him up with someone on the outside?"

"Exactly. I decided to do some research on prisoners with a history of bank robbery. Of course there were plenty of those. Then I cross checked that list with prisoners who were released or paroled around the same time that Karl left his job."

"Samantha, you are a genius!" Eddy could barely contain his excitement. "What did you find?"

"Well, there were a few people that were released around the same time. Unfortunately, none of them had a history of bank robbery, but that doesn't mean they aren't potentially involved. So, right now I have someone with the parole department looking into those that were paroled within a couple of months of Karl's transition to the bank. Sorry it's not more conclusive, but it's just a hunch I am following."

"It's a great hunch, Samantha, I never would have thought of it. I guess by tomorrow we should have some more information to go on."

"I sure hope so," Samantha said eagerly. "We're not getting very far, so far."

"Hey, it's farther than Detective Brunner, who isn't even looking into the case properly." Eddy rolled his eyes. "Politics apparently."

"All right, well call me in the morning and let me know if you find out anything."

"Same for you." Eddy walked her to the door. "Samantha, it's great that you're helping with this. I just can't rest until this is solved."

"Eddy, I have to admit, this is one of the best birthday gifts I have ever received." Samantha laughed. "Good night."

"Good night." Eddy watched as Samantha walked down the path towards her villa until he was sure that she was safe.

Chapter Seven

The next morning Eddy went straight over to Walt's. The one good thing about Walt's early bedtime was that it meant he also woke up very early. Eddy found him drinking his tea on his porch as always.

"Morning Walt."

Walt sipped his tea and watched Eddy over the brim of the mug. When he set the mug down he gestured for Eddy to join him. "I guess this early visit means that you've got something for me?"

"Yes, I do. These are Karl's phone records." Eddy slid a folder towards him. "Also, you should know that Samantha thinks it is possible that he might have bonded with one of the inmates in the prison where he worked. That might be the reason why he quit his job at the prison and took the job at the bank. He might have planned the entire thing and positioned himself as the security guard to make sure that nothing went wrong."

"That's a lot of 'might haves'," Walt said as he picked up the folder and began scanning the papers inside. "I did some initial research last night," Walt explained without taking his eyes off the papers. "He would have taken a big pay cut when he left the prison and became a security guard."

"Exactly." Eddy nodded. "I think that alone indicates something was off. There aren't too many people that are going to willingly lose out on that much income."

"Yes, but it doesn't prove anything," Walt said.

"Hopefully, you'll find something in his phone records."

"Yes, yes. Hopefully." Walt tapped the folder lightly against the table top. "However, it will take me some time to go through the phone numbers and see if there is a pattern."

"How long do you need?" Eddy met Walt's

eyes. "The longer we take to solve the case the less chance of finding any potential evidence."

"My work can't be rushed, Eddy. You know that. However, I understand the urgency and I will keep you updated about whatever I find. All right?"

"All right." Eddy sighed. A part of him had hoped that Walt could simply look at the numbers and find Karl's contact. Then he could go to Detective Brunner with his findings and the robber and murderer would be found. "I'm going to look into a few things while you work your magic. Expect a call from Samantha, as I'm sure she'll want an update on your progress."

"I wouldn't expect anything less." Walt chuckled. He picked up his mug of tea, and the folder. "I'll see what I can dig up."

Eddy left Walt's and headed back to his villa. He called Samantha along the way.

"I didn't hear anything back from the parole board yet, Eddy."

"I figured it was a bit early for the parole department." Eddy chuckled. "That's not the only reason I was calling."

"What's up? Did Walt find something already?"

"Not yet. I need some information from you actually. There's a teller at the bank, her name is Terry. She is Paul Carlil's granddaughter. Can you find her address for me?"

"That depends, will this be a personal visit, or a work visit?" Eddy could hear the teasing in Samantha's voice.

"It's a work visit, Samantha. I want to talk to her about what she saw at the bank that day, and whether she knows anything about Karl. I'm not convinced that she's not somehow involved in all of this."

"Everyone's a suspect, hmm? I'll call you back."

"Thanks."

***

Eddy headed for his car. He didn't know how Terry would react to some customer hunting her down, but he was at the point of not caring. He knew that time was ticking and he hoped the fact that he lived in the same community as her grandfather would make her trust him more. Eddy couldn't let a crime that had unfolded right in front of him go unsolved.

He was already driving in the direction of the bank when his phone rang. Samantha had set up something in his car that allowed the phone to be projected through the speakers of his radio. He was jolted by the sound of her voice all around him.

"Eddy, are you there?"

"I'm here. Can you hear me?"

"Yes, you don't have to shout."

"Okay, sorry."

"It's okay," Samantha said. "I haven't spoken to the parole board yet, but I did speak to a friend at the bank Karl Connell uses, and apparently he recently paid off a large portion of his mortgage. Cash payment apparently."

"Wow," Eddy said with surprise. "Good work. It could just be a coincidence. But it could also be related to the robbery."

"Seems like a big coincidence to me. I also have the address that you asked me for."

Eddy pulled the car over to the side of the road so that he could write down the address. He knew the street.

"Thanks Samantha."

"No problem. Just don't get yourself arrested, Eddy."

"I'll try not to." After a few tries Eddy figured out how to hang up the phone.

He drove to the address. The closer he got the more apprehensive he became. When he had a badge questioning random people was not a problem, but now that he was retired he didn't have that authority. With the way Detective Brunner acted, he doubted that the man would stand up for him if he got into trouble. He could only hope that the woman would be friendly enough to talk to him. He parked a few houses down from the address and got out to walk. He didn't want to scare her off. As Eddy walked up to the driveway he noticed that she was outside unlocking the door of her car. Eddy cleared his throat.

"Excuse me, miss?" She opened the door to her car. Eddy knew that if she got in, his chance to speak to her would vanish. "Terry?"

She turned to look at him with a touch of recognition in her expression. "I'm sorry, do I know you?"

Eddy's ego was a little deflated. It wasn't as if he had expected her to be in love with him, but at the very least she could remember his face. He had been going to the same bank at least once a week for years. Since she had started working there he always tried to make sure that he was in her line because she was friendly to him. He recovered from his injured pride as quickly as possible.

"You probably don't know who I am, but I was at the bank the day it was robbed."

"Oh." She nodded. Then she smiled. "Oh, you must be one of the bank's customers then."

"Yes." Eddy cleared his throat. He found it a little strange that it appeared as if she didn't know who he was. She had told her grandfather about him, so she must have had some idea, but maybe the stress from the robbery clouded her recollection. "You have helped me several times. I was wondering if you could give me a little information."

"Information about what?" She narrowed her eyes. Eddy was aware that she felt uncomfortable.

"About the security guard, Karl?" He watched her reaction to the name. Her eyes widened just enough to show the whites of her eyes.

"Oh, I don't really know him very well." She frowned and started to move to get into her car.

"No?" Eddy decided not to mention that he

had seen her chasing after him. "How long have you two worked together?"

"Well, we didn't. I mean, I worked behind the counter and he worked security." She seemed annoyed. "Like I said, we barely had a conversation."

"I understand that. But wasn't he there with you at opening and closing?" Eddy found her evasiveness to be a little unsettling.

"Sure he was, but he mainly worked with the manager. I didn't really have anything to do with that." Again she started to slide into the front seat of her car. Eddy stood back so that she could. He made it seem as if he was about to walk away, then caught the door before she could close it.

"So, you don't know anything about any other friends he might have had at the bank?"

"I don't understand why you are asking me all of these questions." Terry seemed downright irritated. "Are you a police officer or something? Can't you just ask Karl yourself?"

"I'm just trying to find out why he acted so strangely at the robbery. You know, I thought he would try to stop the robbery, instead he seemed happy to let the robber go." Eddy leaned in towards Terry. "Don't you find that odd?"

"Do I find it odd that he did what a crazy man with a gun told him to?" She glared at Eddy. "No I don't. I did the same thing, didn't I? I made sure he got everything from my drawer. If he had asked me to stand on my head and sing the alphabet I would have. What I do find odd is you showing up in my driveway to ask me questions about a bank robbery when you are not a police officer. In fact, I find it strange enough that I intend to report it to the actual police. If you don't let go of my door I will be calling them right now." She whipped out her cell phone.

Eddy took a step back. He remembered Samantha's warning about not getting arrested. He began wishing he had asked her to join him. She was much better at talking to people than he was. She had a way of putting everyone at ease.

"I'm sorry to bother you, Terry. Just remember that if it's an inside job, the sooner the truth is told, the better off everyone is."

"How dare you!" She slammed her door closed without the slightest concern for Eddy's fingertips. Eddy managed to release the door just before his hand would have been caught. Terry roared out of the driveway. Eddy was left in a cloud of exhaust fumes and pollen. He waved his hand in front of his face and willed himself not to sneeze.

"Well, that did not go well." He frowned. The one thing he felt he had accomplished was ensuring that Terry would never speak to him again. He guessed he would be lucky if he wasn't banned from the bank, which would be very inconvenient as it was the only branch in the area. As he trudged back towards his car, his phone began to ring. He was relieved to see that it was Walt. He hoped that he would have some good news for him.

"I have something for you." Walt sounded

quite proud of himself. Eddy couldn't help but smile at his tone.

"What is it?" He started the car. He wanted to be able to make a quick getaway in case Terry really had called the police.

"Well, I looked through the phone records you gave me."

"And?" Eddy pressed.

"There was one particular number that Karl called often since the robbery. From what I can tell the first time Karl called the number was shortly after the robbery," Walt explained. "The first and only time he received a call from this number was on the day he stopped working at the prison. The number is registered to a person named Charlie Deloney."

"Wow." Eddy was impressed. "How did you figure all of that out so fast?"

"Do I ask you how you get that cop look that makes people confess anything you ask them to?"

"Cop look? I don't have a cop look."

Eddy pulled the phone away from his ear as Walt laughed loudly into it. "Okay, if you say so. Do you want Charlie's address?"

"Yes please." Eddy pulled out his notebook and jotted down Charlie's address right under Terry's. "Thanks Walt." He hung up the phone. Eddy stared at the address for a moment. Seeing Terry's address reminded him of Samantha, and how much better she was at talking to people than he was. He had regretted not having her with him when he spoke to Terry. He dialed her number.

"Hello? Did you talk to Terry?"

"Yes, I did. I didn't get very much information though. Are you dressed?"

"Am I dressed? What kind of question is that? Of course I'm dressed."

"Okay, I'll be there in fifteen minutes to pick you up."

"Oh. Okay." Her tone became eager. "I'll be here."

Eddy smiled at her enthusiasm. She could

make even the most tedious investigation feel like an adventure.

Chapter Eight

When Eddy pulled into Samantha's driveway, his cell phone began to ring.

"I'm here, Samantha, I'm right out front."

"Eddy, it's Detective Brunner."

Eddy snapped to attention. "Oh Detective, sorry. Have you found out something about the robbery?"

"No. Actually, I might be forced to open an entirely different case."

"What's that?"

"A stalking case, and you would be the prime suspect."

"Ouch."

"Yes ouch. That's exactly how I felt when I was told that the bank teller had reported she was being harassed by you. You're lucky I snatched the case up before it could get filed. You need to stay away from Terry Carlil, do you understand?"

"Yes, I understand." Eddy frowned. He didn't think he'd get any more information out of her anyway. If she was willing to go to the police then she wasn't likely involved in the robbery. He sighed as yet another suspect was crossed off his list.

"Eddy, I know that you're determined to look into this investigation. But there are procedures that have to be followed. So, before you go getting yourself tangled up in something you can't get out of, just think about the consequences."

"Will do, Detective." Eddy quickly hung up the phone. He stared down at it for a moment, then shook his head. Samantha opened the passenger door just as he did.

"You all right?" She frowned as she sat down in the car. "You look like you just got caught with your hand in the cookie jar."

"Maybe I did." Eddy laughed a little. "Let's just say we can't expect too much support from Detective Brunner."

"Well, that's no surprise. He's awfully green."

"That's one way of putting it." Eddy turned on the engine. "Although, I'm starting to wonder if it's just youth, or that he really doesn't care about this case."

"Detective Brunner?"

"From the get go on this case he's been dropping the ball. I don't know, it just makes me wonder."

Samantha frowned. "Do you really think he'd be intentionally sabotaging the case?"

"I don't know." Eddy gazed out through the windshield. "I don't want to think it."

"What motive could he have?" Samantha's brow furrowed.

"Have you ever seen a detective's paycheck, Samantha? It's not pretty." Eddy's hands tightened on the steering wheel. "I just hope it's not the case."

"We'll just have to keep our eyes and ears open. Until we have proof, we have to give him the benefit of the doubt."

"You're right." Eddy shifted the car into reverse.

"Where are we going?" Samantha looked over her shoulder.

"Walt gave me a lead on someone that Karl started calling often just after the robbery and the only time the person called him was the day he left the prison. It might be nothing, but I think it's worth looking into. Maybe it's the same person that paid off some of his mortgage. If someone directed him to get a job at the bank, then they might have supplemented his income."

"That would explain the move." Samantha nodded.

"The name is Charlie Deloney. Other than that I don't have any information on him. It might just be a coincidence, but if our theory is correct and Karl was coerced into assisting with the robbery then it's definitely worth looking into. Someone with that much influence could be a very dangerous man." He accelerated just a little past the speed limit. He wanted to get to the address and see if they could prove their theory.

"Honestly, if we are correct, whoever came up with a plan like this must have been a mastermind. Let me check and see if Charlie Deloney is associated with any of the prisoners that were recently paroled." As she chatted on the phone with someone she knew from the parole department, Eddy maneuvered his way through traffic. By the time Samantha hung up the phone he pulled the car to a stop in front of a house.

"Dead end with the parole department." Samantha tucked her phone back into her purse.

"This is the address." Eddy gripped the steering wheel tightly. He glanced over at Samantha. Even though she was a capable and intelligent person, he had difficulty with putting her at any kind of risk. "Should I bother asking you to stay in the car?"

"You can ask," she said as she opened the car door.

Eddy got out of the car and looked at the small house. With its peeling paint and untended garden it certainly didn't scream bank robber. But Eddy knew that didn't mean anything. He followed Samantha towards the house.

"So remember, we're going to scope it out. No accusations."

"I have plenty of experience getting information out of people, Eddy. Remember?" She smiled sweetly at him. He wasn't sure that he had ever seen a more dangerous expression. He followed right behind her on the way to the house. As they walked past the car in the driveway Eddy instinctively peered inside. There was nothing on the backseat aside from a few empty, paper coffee cups. When they reached the front door Samantha knocked, then glanced over her shoulder at Eddy. Eddy nodded to reassure her just as the door swung open.

"May I help you?" The woman's face was distorted by the old, dusty screen in the storm door. However, Eddy assessed her as being in her mid-thirties with short, brown hair.

"Hi. I'm so sorry to bother you. We're looking

for Charlie." Samantha turned her charming smile on the woman.

"Who are you?"

Eddy braced himself. The woman was not denying that she knew any Charlie, but she was clearly suspicious about why they were there.

Eddy's strength was in interrogation and brute force, something he didn't want to use in this situation. He hoped that Samantha would be able to come up with something to get them in the door, or at least a lead to where Charlie might be.

"I just want to speak to Charlie," Samantha said with a smile.

"Oh, is that so?" The woman leaned forward on the door which made it creak open. "About what?"

"We're old friends and I just want to talk to him, catch up."

"You're old friends with Charlie?"

"Yes."

Eddy sensed that something was off. "Could

you just let us know where we might be able to find him?"

"Well, that depends."

"Depends on what?" Samantha asked.

"It depends on whether you are looking for Charlie or you are looking for a man."

"What?" Eddy said as he exchanged a quick glance with Samantha.

"I think you two should leave." She let go of the screen door and it banged shut. The heavy, wooden door banged shut right behind it. Eddy heard the click of a lock being turned into place.

"It seems like she's not the talkative type." Samantha shook her head.

"She might not be, but she knows Charlie." Eddy passed his gaze over the house again. "It's a small place. If she lives with him, she's probably a wife or a girlfriend. She's going to cover for him."

"So, is it a loss?" Samantha frowned.

"No, I think we should stakeout the house." Eddy gestured towards the street. "Let's give her some space. Charlie is going to want to come home, eventually."

"Good idea." Samantha nodded. The two walked casually back to the car.

"Let's pick up some supplies then we'll come back here and keep an eye on the house."

Eddy held the door open for Samantha. Once she was settled he closed it. When he turned on the car, he noticed a flutter of the curtains in the house. The woman was watching to make sure that they left.

"Are you sure that she knows Charlie?"

Eddy nodded. "She knows him all right and if we watch the house we'll find him."

***

After Eddy and Samantha had stocked up on chips, soda, and magazines they drove back towards the house.

"Pull in there." Samantha gestured to a coffee shop. "I'll get us a coffee."

"Thanks," Eddy said as he pulled up outside

the shop. He hadn't even noticed it from the road. Eddy watched as Samantha walked into the small coffee shop. Eddy laughed to himself as he thought of how different it was doing a stakeout with someone like Samantha as opposed to one of his old partners. She always ensured that they were well-nourished no matter what the circumstances were. Samantha walked out shortly after with two cups of coffee.

"All set," she said as she opened the door.

"Thanks." Eddy took his cup from her. He noticed that the cup had the same design as the cups on the backseat of the car at Charlie's house. He guessed that Charlie might be a regular.

Eddy drove back to Charlie's house which was at the end of the street. He parked the car a few houses down. It gave him a clear view of the driveway, but enough distance that the woman would not be able to see the car.

"How long do you think it will be?" Samantha thumbed through a magazine, but her eyes were locked on the house.

"Don't know." Eddy continued to stare out through the windshield. He had a tendency to get tunnel vision on a stakeout.

"I hope it's not too long." Samantha sighed and leaned her head back against the seat. "Stakeouts were always my least favorite part of an investigation."

"Sometimes I forget that you had to do so many of the same things I did. Interesting isn't it? Our careers were so different, but some of the tasks were so similar."

"I don't think our careers were as different as you think. There were many times that I stopped a crime, and many times you did."

"Maybe so, but I never got a prisoner out of jail." Eddy cleared his throat. An awkward silence fell between them. Samantha's advocacy for wrongfully convicted criminals was a tense subject between them. The quiet shattered when she chomped down on a chip. A moment later a car rolled down the street and then turned into Charlie's driveway. As the car drove past them

Eddy noticed a man inside that could have easily met the description of the robber. Since he had not seen the robber's face it was hard to say for sure, but the build was similar enough for him to want to check it out.

"I'm going to get closer so I can see who is getting out of the car."

"You're not leaving me here." Samantha frowned.

"Listen, I get that you're a strong and liberated woman, Samantha, but you're also an experienced investigator, which means that you know two people can make a lot more commotion and risk being exposed than one." He raised an eyebrow. "Can you argue with that?"

Samantha opened her mouth as if she was thinking about attempting to. Then she closed her mouth again. She shook her head. Eddy's lips curled upward as he savored a rare triumph, then he opened the car door and stepped out.

"The keys are still in the ignition. If anything goes haywire get out of here, understand?"

Samantha nodded, but she didn't meet his eyes. Eddy had no doubt that she would not leave him behind, no matter what happened.

Chapter Nine

Eddy made his way along the front sidewalk as quietly as he could. With the limitations of his body he was no longer as lithe as he had once been. But flexibility had never been his strong suit. Using force to stop a criminal from hurting someone was. He summoned all of his finesse as he heard a car door slam shut. Eddy ducked back behind a tree as the man approached the front door. It only took him a moment to recognize who it was. It was not who he had expected, and also not the bank robber. The man banged on the front door.

"Charlie!" He shouted.

Eddy knew that he was the security guard from the bank, Karl. He was looking for Charlie, which meant that there was indeed a connection between the two of them. However, that didn't explain everything. Especially when the door swung open and the woman that Eddy had spoken to earlier stepped out.

"Stop making such a racket. Do you think that we need the attention of everyone in the neighborhood?" Her voice dripped with fury.

"You're not returning my calls!"

"I warned you to stop calling me. You should never have come here." She looked towards the road. Eddy ducked further behind the tree and hoped that he hadn't been spotted. "Did anyone see you?"

"No. No one saw me. Charlie, things are getting out of hand."

Charlie? Eddy peeked around the side of the tree. Only then did it strike him that a female could be named Charlie as well. The thought had never occurred to him and they had been in too much of a hurry for Samantha to have the chance to do any proper research. Eddy felt a mixture of relief and confusion. They had found Charlie, but she clearly was not the robber. Neither was the security guard that was still arguing with her.

"You need to go home. Go home and turn off your phone. Turn off your television. Everything is going to be just fine. But you have to disconnect from the chaos."

"But, Charlie please…"

"Go home," she growled. Eddy could hear the fury in her voice. He knew that she was not making a suggestion, but forcibly instructing him to go home.

The two stared hard at each other for a moment. Eddy half-expected a fight to break out. Instead Karl hung his head. He turned and walked back to his car. It was clear that Charlie had won the battle. She remained outside the door with her arms folded across her chest until Karl backed all the way out of the driveway. Only then did she go back into the house. Eddy continued to wait a few minutes longer just in case she was peering out the window. Once he thought the coast was clear he headed back to the car. Samantha popped open the driver's side door for him. Eddy settled into the seat and then turned to meet her eyes.

"Well?" She smiled with the kind of eagerness that only a journalist could have. "Did you find out anything?"

"I found out that Charlie is not a man."

"What?" Samantha laughed. When his expression didn't change her eyes widened. "Wait, are you serious?"

"Yup. The woman that answered the door was Charlie all along. That isn't even the best part." He paused, as he knew she enjoyed a little drama.

"What is it?" Samantha demanded.

"The person who came to visit her was Karl, the security guard. They are definitely working together." Samantha stared at Eddy for a moment as she processed the information.

"Can we call Detective Brunner to pick them up?"

"No, I don't think that would be a good idea. I heard enough for me to be suspicious, but they didn't really say anything incriminating. If we send Brunner in too soon then they will be tipped off and we may never find out the truth." Eddy decided not to remind her that he was already on very thin ice with Detective Brunner.

"What is the truth, what do you think?" Samantha looked over at him as he drove towards Sage Gardens.

"I think that there is a much bigger team than we first thought. When we first discovered Charlie I was sure that he had to be the bank robber. Then he turned out to be a she. So, if the robber was not Charlie, and obviously the robber is not the security guard, then who is he?"

"Could he be the man they found dead?" Samantha sat back and tapped her fingers against the dashboard. "Maybe he was the robber and he was teamed up with Charlie, but Charlie wanted him to take the fall."

"It's possible." Eddy nodded. "I guess I need to find out more about the man they found dead."

"I think we should keep an eye on Charlie, too." Samantha pulled out her phone. "I can do some deeper research into her."

"Well, I think I know where to start. I think I

know where she likes to get coffee from."

"Really? Where?" Samantha's eyes widened.

"The place we went to this morning. Charlie had coffee cups on her backseat and I remember Karl holding a coffee cup when I walked into the bank. I can't remember what the name on it was, but it looked very similar," he said as he held up the coffee cup from the coffee Samantha had bought him. "Maybe they went to the same place? Maybe they met there? If she's a creature of habit, she'll likely use it as a meeting place again. I know it's a stretch, but it's worth a shot. Why don't we stakeout that area? We can do some more research from the car."

"Great, I'm starving. These snacks did not cut it."

Eddy laughed as he changed direction and drove the car towards the coffee shop. His laughter faded however as he wondered what it would mean if the dead man was not the robber either. Would that mean that there was a fourth person involved in all of this?

Once he was parked at the coffee shop, Samantha headed inside to get them both some food. While she was inside Eddy was looking out his window at the park across the road from the shop. There were a few kids playing ball. One kid picked up the ball and Eddy watched as he threw it with his left hand. It reminded him that the robber was left-handed. Eddy placed a call to Chris. As soon as the line was answered Eddy spoke. He didn't want Chris to stop him from asking what he needed to.

"I just need one more favor, buddy."

"Chris is not doing you any more favors." Detective Brunner's voice was not what Eddy had expected to hear.

"Oh uh." Eddy's heart raced. He wasn't sure how he was going to talk himself out of this one. "Detective, I was just about to call you."

"Funny, because I got the feeling you were trying to keep me in the dark about what you have been up to."

"Would I do something like that?" Eddy

chuckled. He tried to hide his own suspicion of Detective Brunner. Yet again he was throwing a wrench in the works.

"This is no laughing matter, Eddy. You're getting yourself into a bad position. You're using police resources for unauthorized purposes?"

"Listen Detective, I have a question for you. The man that you found dead, you're saying that he was the bank robber, correct?"

"I'm not saying it, the proof is saying it and it is the best lead we've got, he was found with money from the robbery."

"I understand that. Is there a way to tell if he was left-handed or right-handed?"

"The medical examiner recorded him as being right-handed. Why?"

"Because the robber that I saw held his gun in his left hand."

"Eddy, that doesn't necessarily mean anything. You could have been mistaken, or he could have had a reason to hold the gun in his left hand."

"Have you ever known anyone to use their left hand to hold their weapon if they are right-handed?" Eddy grew impatient. He knew that Detective Brunner was a young detective who was still finding his way, but the way he investigated the case could be frustrating. "Detective, are you in the business of solving crimes or closing cases for the sake of your superior? Because you need to decide now what kind of detective you are going to be. Are you going to be by the book or are you going to be by justice?"

"That's not really a fair way of putting it." Detective Brunner's voice wavered.

"All right, then you tell me right now that you believe the man that you found in that house was the same man that robbed the bank and was the only robber involved. You tell me right now that you are certain of that, and comfortable with moving on from this case."

Eddy was so worked up that he barely noticed Samantha when she opened the door.

"I can't know that for certain." Detective Brunner sounded reluctant.

"Then you haven't solved anything, have you?" Eddy's voice was laced with anger. "So, are you satisfied with that? Are you going to tell me that you will ignore the information of an eye witness to a crime for the sake of not ruffling any feathers?"

"Eddy, that's not what I'm saying, but there are rules and you are very aware of their importance. You are no longer an active member of the police force..."

"Well, this non-active member of the police force is about to solve a crime that you and your police force have decided to neglect, Detective Brunner." Eddy hung up the phone. As a rule he did not normally antagonize his connections. He did his best not to let his emotions get in the way. However, the disappointment he felt in Detective Brunner's behavior was enough to make him go against his own rule. It was more than disappointment. It seemed to Eddy that Detective

Brunner worked against him every step of the way. Why would he do that?

"You okay?" Samantha frowned and offered him a french fry. "He's just trying to do his job you know."

"No, I don't know that." Eddy took the fry and bit down on it hard. "His job is to protect the people of this community, how is he doing that if he does not solve the crime?"

"Give him time, Eddy. We can't all be as courageous or stubborn as you." Samantha winked at him. Eddy tried not to smile, but he did anyway. Samantha could always get him to lighten up.

"You're right." He sighed. "I got too caught up in all of this. I just hate to think of Charlie and whoever else she's connected to getting away with it."

"Don't worry, she won't. Eat your food and relax. We might have a long stakeout ahead of us. I spoke to my connection on the parole board, and even though Charlie herself does not have a record of any kind, her name popped up on a list of known associates of someone who was recently paroled from the prison where Karl worked." Samantha's eyes glowed with pride. "How's that for connecting the dots?"

"Wow! Did you get a name?"

"I did, the name is Derek Quinns. He doesn't have a history of violence so I don't think he's the murderer, but he does have a history of breaking and entering. It's not bank robbery, but it's still criminal behavior."

"Sounds like that might be our guy. Now, I know that the man who was killed was not the man in the bank, because the man in the bank was left-handed."

"Do you remember anything else about the man?" Samantha met his eyes. "Any distinguishing marks of any kind?"

Eddy closed his eyes. "You're not hypnotizing me again." He opened one eye to be sure.

"I'm not." She laughed and held up her hands.

"Okay, I remember seeing the gun in his left hand."

"How did you notice it? What drew your attention?" Samantha leaned a little closer. Her voice became soothing.

"Watch it." Eddy opened both eyes. "I noticed a glimmer of the gun. It caught the light."

"The gun did?" Samantha looked skeptical. "Are you sure?"

"Yes," Eddy said. "It was definitely in his left hand."

"Okay, so we know the murdered man is right-handed and the robber is left-handed." Samantha smiled.

"We know something else, too. Charlie is a creature of habit." Eddy tilted his head towards the parking lot. "There she is."

"Wow, that was fast." Samantha slid down in her seat some. They watched as the woman lingered by the entrance of the coffee shop. Eddy pulled out a small set of binoculars to get a closer look.

"Okay, she's going in."

Samantha leaned forward and peered through the windshield. The small coffee shop was easy to miss from the road. It looked like it was mainly a local spot, which was probably why Charlie chose it.

"Let's give her a minute and make sure she doesn't come back out." Eddy lowered his binoculars.

"I think that she must be waiting for someone in there." Samantha watched the parking lot. "Let's see if anyone else shows up."

Eddy's cell phone began to ring. He was flustered by the sound of it because he was focusing on the coffee shop. He looked at it quickly. "It's Jo."

"Answer, she probably just wants to check in."

"Why?" Eddy met Samantha's eyes. "Did you tell her we were doing this?"

Samantha avoided looking directly at him.

"Maybe."

"Maybe?" Eddy raised an eyebrow. He continued to look in her direction as he answered the phone. "Hi Jo."

"Hey Eddy. I tried calling Samantha, but it was going straight to voicemail."

"Do you have your phone turned off?" Eddy gestured to Samantha's purse.

"Oops, I do, I wonder how I did that." She frowned with frustration and turned the phone back on.

"Sorry, she had it off. She's turning it on now if you want to call her."

"No, that's okay. I just wanted to make sure you two were all right."

Eddy smiled at the idea of Jo worrying about him. She was not the type to show concern. "We're fine. In fact, hopefully we'll know who the actual robber was soon. I assume Samantha has filled you in?"

"Maybe."

Eddy looked over at Samantha with annoyance. He wondered if all women had the same list of responses to choose from.

"Well, we're waiting for the next move. We'll update you when we get the chance."

"Be careful, Eddy."

"I will." He hung up the phone and looked sternly at Samantha. "Stakeouts are need to know, you know."

"She needed to know. Just like Walt did."

Eddy nodded silently. He understood that Samantha didn't want Jo to be left out. He noticed movement near the front of the coffee shop. A man who looked like he could match the build of the robber paused in front of the door. He glanced back over his shoulder, offering Eddy a full view of his face. Eddy had never seen him before, but there was something familiar about the way he carried himself.

"I bet that's the robber."

"What makes you think that? Is there

something you recognize?" Samantha leaned forward.

"I just think it's him. Shall we get some coffee?" He opened the car door.

"Are you sure?" Samantha frowned. "We don't want to blow our cover."

"We're not going to get anywhere if we don't hear what they are talking about." Eddy met her eyes. "If it's too risky for you, don't do it."

"Please, risk is not an issue for me." She opened her car door. As they started to walk up towards the coffee shop, Eddy reached out and took her hand in his. Samantha looked over at him with some surprise.

"It'll help us blend in," he muttered. Samantha gave his hand a little squeeze.

"I'm not complaining." She winked at him. Eddy stared at her for a moment and then laughed. He swung open the door of the coffee shop and held it as she stepped inside.

The coffee shop was tiny. It was also very dim.

Eddy was relieved at that. He knew that Charlie had already seen both of their faces and likely suspected they were up to something, so if she spotted them she would bolt. As he suspected they would be, Charlie and the man who had just entered were clustered together at a table in the back. Eddy gestured to a table that was half-hidden by a wall that jutted out from the kitchen. Samantha sat down with Eddy right behind her. A moment later they gave quick and quiet orders for coffee. Eddy kept his eyes on Charlie. Her posture showed that she was in charge. The man across from her had his head bowed as if he was looking for forgiveness. Eddy strained to hear what they were saying.

"People are suspicious," Charlie said. "They've started snooping around."

"Don't worry they have nothing to go on. My source in the police department confirmed it just this morning. Nobody is looking in our direction."

"Don't you try to tell me what you think you know, Derek." Eddy's eyes widened slightly at the mention of the guy's name. This must be Derek Quinns. "It was a simple job that I planned perfectly, and now people are looking for me. That means that someone suspects something. I am not going to go down for this. Understand?"

"What are you trying to say? That you expect me to take the fall for you?"

Eddy listened closer. It was becoming clear to him that Charlie was the mastermind. Derek was certainly a puppet of hers, and it appeared that Karl probably was as well. What he wasn't sure about was how the dead man was linked into all of it. The waitress delivered Eddy and Samantha their coffee, which muffled a few minutes of conversation between Charlie and Derek. Eddy tried to wave the waitress away as fast as he could, but she was more than a little chatty. Once she was gone Samantha shifted in her chair.

"I can't hear anything," Samantha hissed. She was sitting closer to the kitchen and the sound of the coffee grinders surrounded her.

"Sh." Eddy pretended to sip his coffee.

"You're being ridiculous, Charlie." Derek's voice raised an octave. "I did everything you asked me to."

"I'm telling you right now, if you breathe a word of my involvement you will pay a far greater price than going to jail. Got me?" Charlie scowled. "This has got very messy. The police are suspecting us because the guy was murdered."

"That's not my fault!" Derek's voice grew loud. Charlie smacked the table hard.

"Quiet down." She scowled at him.

Derek grimaced and then leaned across the table. He lowered his voice so much that Eddy couldn't hear what he was muttering. Charlie was closer to him so he could still hear most of what she was saying.

"All that matters is that my name stays out of this and I'm not tied to this in any way. If you breathe a word of it, not only will you pay, but I'll make sure you don't see a dime of that money."

"Speaking of the money, when am I going to

see my cut? I stuck to my end of the deal. The dead guy has more money than I do."

"The dead guy doesn't have any money. That was a sacrifice. Once the heat dies down, then you will get your money. Understand?" Charlie said. "I am not risking going to jail because we rush things."

"No one is going to jail. You know?"

"I know I'm not." Charlie glared at him.

Eddy grimaced at the harshness in the woman's tone. He had encountered some cold-hearted criminals in his time, but this woman appeared to have no emotion other than anger. It was amazing to him that it appeared she had orchestrated the entire bank robbery and was also in possession of the remaining funds.

"You just need to relax, Charlie. Everything's fine." Derek cleared his throat.

"What about Karl?"

"What about him?" Derek frowned.

"He's a weak link."

"I told you, he's taken care of."

"You think he is. But maybe we underestimated his intelligence. What if he decides to go to the police?"

"You don't have to worry about him."

"All right, Derek. Fine. I'm going to hold you to that."

"Charlie, you know you can trust me."

"I hope so," Charlie said. "Because if things go sideways, Derek, there will be consequences."

"Don't worry," Derek said as he picked up his coffee cup with his left hand and took a sip. "I'll take care of it. I have to get some sleep before I go to work. I've got the nightshift," he said as he stood up from the table.

"Remember what I said, Derek," Charlie said bitterly. "I will not go down for any of this."

Eddy shook his head slightly. It seemed that Derek was the robber, but Charlie was the ring leader, the real criminal. Samantha started to stand up when she saw Charlie follow Derek out the door.

"Wait." Eddy grabbed her hand and guided her back down into her chair. "We don't want to leave right away. Finish your coffee."

"Are you going to tell me what you heard?"

"Derek's the bank robber, I'm almost sure of it. Charlie is the one with all of the control. Karl, he might be the next one to die." Eddy finished his coffee. "I think we've gotten ourselves in the middle of quite a scheme. Now we need to work out who the murderer is."

"Is it time now to bring in the police?" Samantha frowned.

"Honestly, after the way I spoke to Brunner, I don't think he's going to listen to a thing I have to say. What we need is some solid proof. Like the gun from the murder, or some of the missing money. That's the only way I'm going to get Detective Brunner interested enough to look into Derek and Charlie. It sounds like Derek has connections in the police department who may be pushing the investigation away from him and

Charlie." Eddy thought that his connection might be Brunner, but he didn't want to believe it.

"So, what's our next step?" Samantha finished her coffee as well.

"Let's have a conversation with Jo."

"Oh, I can call her." Samantha pulled out her phone.

"No. Let's go see her. We need to talk in person."

"What are you thinking?" Samantha asked as she sent a text to Jo asking to meet.

Eddy didn't answer, he just drove towards Jo's villa. More than once he had felt conflicted about involving Jo in behavior that wasn't exactly legal. However, of the four of them she was the most likely to be successful in the next stage of his plan. With Detective Brunner angry at him, and his connection to Chris cut off, he needed to be sure that the case was solved or some bridges might be permanently burned.

Chapter Ten

By the time Eddy and Samantha walked up to Jo's villa, she was waiting for them outside the door. She leaned one shoulder up against the doorway and had her arms folded over her chest. Eddy could see the arrogance in her expression. He knew that she had an idea about what he was going to ask her to do.

"What's up guys?" She looked from Samantha to Eddy, then back to Samantha again. Eddy could already tell by the squint of her eyes that she wasn't altogether pleased.

"Can we talk inside?" Eddy asked and gestured towards the door.

"I guess." She opened the door and allowed them to walk through. Jo was not the type to invite people over too often. Once inside she turned to face them. "So, what is it?"

"Listen Jo, you know we're looking into this bank robbery. I'm just wondering if you might be able to help us out." He looked at her with a hint of remorse in his eyes.

"Ah, you need my skills do you?" She winked at Samantha. When she looked back at Eddy she tilted her head to the side. "It's amazing that an old cop like you appreciates my talents now." She smiled.

"All right, all right, don't rub it in. Will you help us or not?"

"Hm. Yup." She laughed a little. "I have nothing better to do. Where and what?"

"It's a man's house. His name is Derek Quinns. We suspect he is the one who actually robbed the bank. But with no proof whatsoever it's going to be difficult to prove that."

"Yes, we overheard him talking to the suspected mastermind of the crime. We're sure he's involved. But we need evidence." Samantha frowned. "Maybe if we can get a look inside of his place, we'll be able to find something."

"I understand." Jo nodded.

"I overheard him saying he's working tonight," Eddy explained.

"I just need a little time to get everything prepared."

"I'll go with you." Eddy spoke with determination.

"Aw." Jo patted Eddy's cheek with a palm slightly roughened by her gardening. "That's sweet, hon, but I work alone."

Eddy narrowed his eyes. Jo was one of very few people that could easily make him feel like he had no ground to stand on. "It's not safe. I'd rather be there to make sure that you're okay."

"I'll be fine. I'll let you know what I find when I find it." She glanced over at Samantha. "You can keep him company until then, right?"

Samantha frowned. "Maybe Eddy's right, Jo. You didn't see this woman. She seemed pretty vicious and seemed to know exactly what she was doing."

"Hmm. A vicious woman. Sounds like we

would get along. I'm not concerned. You came to me to ask for help. If you want me to give it I will, but it's going to be on my terms. I don't want to have to worry about what you're up to, or if you threw your back out, Eddy." She pursed her lips with a hint of amusement in her eyes.

Eddy glared at her. "I'll have you know I've done my fair share of clandestine searches."

"I'm sure in your younger years."

"My younger years?" Eddy took a step towards her. "We're about the same age you know."

"If you say so." Jo's eyes nearly glowed with repressed amusement.

"Jo, stop teasing the poor man." Samantha shook her head. "He's right about this one. This isn't your average crime, this woman appears to be dangerous and cunning and we're taking a big risk by crossing her."

"Okay, okay. If it will make you both happy then fine. Eddy can come inside with me, but I call the shots. Understand?"

Eddy tried not to think that Jo sounded a bit similar to Charlie. "Understood." Eddy nodded.

"Let me get some things together. We can go around eleven," Jo said.

"I'll get his address." Samantha sent a text.

"In the meantime we should probably update Walt," Eddy said.

"Yes please."

All three turned to see Walt standing in Jo's doorway.

"Walt, what are you doing here?" Eddy stepped aside to give him more room.

"I just came to see if Jo had heard anything from the two of you, since I am obviously not being kept up-to-date." He chuckled.

"Hey, I was on my way." Eddy clapped his shoulder. Walt shied away from him.

"Eddy," Walt said reproachfully. "I've told you not to hit my shoulder, please."

"Sorry," Eddy frowned. "Thanks to your great work I think we may really be on to something."

"I'm glad I could help." Walt smiled. "Now, what's this you're planning for tonight?"

"I'm going to do a little old fashioned breaking and entering," Jo said.

"What do you mean?" Walt looked directly at Eddy. "You're asking her to break in somewhere?"

"Yes, the home of the man I believe is the actual bank robber and is possibly involved in the murder. She won't be in there long, and she won't be in there alone, I'm going in with her."

"Against my better judgment," Jo said.

"Well, I think it's a terrible idea, does anybody care about that?" Walt glared between the group.

"Why do you think it's a terrible idea?" Jo frowned.

"Because, for one we're breaking into someone's home, which is grounds for arrest. So, let's just assume that Derek was involved in the robbery and possibly the murder. If he was then he is a dangerous man. How can we let Jo just break into someone's home who is clearly a danger?" Walt shook his head. "It's reckless. It's ridiculous."

"It's my choice." Jo narrowed her eyes. "I have no problem with breaking in. I am as invested in this community as all of you are, and I want this guy caught. The residents are going to be living in fear if they think these kinds of criminals are their neighbors."

"Wait, wait. You guys are missing the point. All of this can be done safely if we work together. Eddy can go in with Jo, Walt and I can be lookouts, that way there will be plenty of warning if Derek is coming home. Let's just work together instead of arguing with each other." Samantha smiled with satisfaction. "It's a team effort, right?"

"I don't know." Jo frowned. "In my experience the more people involved in a break-in, the bigger the risk of being caught."

"Let's not bring up your experience." Eddy

cleared his throat.

"And why not? It's why I'm the one to go in and take a look, isn't it?" Jo crossed her arms.

"Enough." Samantha stepped between them. "We all do this together, or we don't do it at all, okay? That way we all assume the risk, and we are all available to watch each other's backs."

Walt nodded. "I'm in."

"It's fine with me," Eddy agreed.

Everyone looked at Jo. She pursed her lips but nodded. "Fine. But I am in charge inside the house, Eddy, don't try to pull any of that cop stuff on me."

"Wouldn't dream of it, Jo." Eddy smirked.

Samantha cringed at the banter between the two. Eddy offered a faint smile of reassurance. He gave Jo a harder time than he needed to. He knew that she had changed quite a bit since her days as a professional cat burglar.

"Let's plan it out and make sure we have all of our angles covered." Walt gestured to Jo. "You can help me figure it out."

"I've got the address. We might be able to get some good information on how to get in if we search it on the internet." As Samantha started to follow after them, Eddy shook his head. Samantha caught the movement out of the corner of her eye.

"What's wrong?" She looked at him with some concern. "Did you think of something that will be a problem?"

"No, I was just thinking it's a good thing we're the good guys."

Samantha laughed a little and nodded. "Just remember that, Eddy. We are the good guys, all of us."

Eddy nodded. "I know."

Chapter Eleven

Once the plans had been set the four gathered for a few more minutes in Jo's living room.

"So, we'll all meet here at around ten-thirty. By then everything should be ready to go." Walt smoothed down his sweater. "I know that this is not normally something I would be involved in, but I'll feel a lot more comfortable being part of it. I just want to make sure that everything goes off without a hitch."

"So do I." Jo smiled. "By tomorrow morning I should be enjoying my garden, and Derek, Charlie, and Karl, should all be enjoying a jail cell."

"Let's hope so." Eddy rubbed his hands together. "If Detective Brunner still refuses to look into these guys even with evidence, then I'm going to have to give up on him."

"Just be patient. He's young." Samantha patted his forearm. "I know that it's hard to remember what it was like when you had to follow the rules, Eddy, but Detective Brunner still has to do that."

"Rules are there for a reason," Walt reminded them as he opened the door for Samantha. "Let's all make sure that we only break the necessary ones."

Eddy decided not to point out that it didn't exactly work that way. Walt was showing a little more flexibility about things and he didn't want him to backslide into being a stickler once more.

"I'll take you home." Eddy offered his arm to Samantha.

"That's all right. I might take a walk down by the water and sort through some things first."

"All right." Eddy nodded. He tried not to be disappointed. He enjoyed hearing Samantha's perspective on things.

He still wasn't sure how the dead man was involved and most importantly who the murderer was, but he was almost completely sure that

Derek was the robber. But that wouldn't matter to Brunner. He would need cold, hard evidence, so that was where their focus needed to remain.

As Eddy walked to his villa he felt a sense of anxiety building within him. As usual he was the one tugging all of his friends into a risky situation. He wondered sometimes if his presence in their lives was more of a nuisance than a benefit. He pushed the thought out of his mind as he reached the walkway to his door. He froze at the bottom of it. Someone was standing by his front door. From behind he couldn't tell exactly who it was.

"Hello?" He took a few steps closer. The man turned to face him with a faint smile.

"Hi. You probably don't know who I am."

Eddy's heart skipped a beat. He knew exactly who he was. But he didn't dare reveal that.

"Should I?" His heart pounded hard against his chest as he looked into Karl Connell's eyes. Had they been caught?

"I was the security guard at the bank. Where

the robbery took place." He searched Eddy's eyes intently. "I just had a couple of questions that I was hoping I could ask you."

"Me?" Eddy cleared his throat. "Why?"

"Well, one of the officers mentioned that you were retired from the police force. I know that you chased after the robber. I just thought you might be able to help me with something." He reached up and rubbed the back of his neck. "I've had a hard time dealing with the robbery."

"Oh?" Eddy did not move any closer.

"Yes. I mean, at the time, it was like I was numb. But ever since, I've just been having these flashes." He shook his head. "You know what I mean?"

"Not exactly." Eddy eyed him with suspicion. He doubted very much that Karl had found him by luck. Which meant that Karl had to be on to the fact that Eddy was on to him. "What are you really doing here, Karl?"

"Oh, so you do know who I am?" The

frightened act faded fast and was replaced by a dark glare. "Amazing how you suddenly remember my name."

Eddy realized his mistake, but it was far too late to correct it. "Karl, I don't know what you think you're going to gain by showing up at my door, but you should know that I have no problem with calling the police."

"I know that." Karl slid his hands deep into his pockets. "That's why I'm here."

"What do you mean?" Eddy was more confused than ever.

"I need your help. Well, more specifically, I need the help of the police. But you're the closest I can get without being locked away."

"How could I possibly help you?" Eddy shook his head. "I don't understand."

"Maybe we should take this conversation inside. I don't know if I've been followed." Karl turned towards the door. Eddy's chest tightened as he realized the decision he had to make. He could invite Karl inside and risk being alone with him, or he could refuse and risk Derek or Charlie witnessing their conversation.

Eddy glanced over his shoulder towards the road. There wasn't a soul in sight. But he knew that didn't mean that Karl hadn't been followed. He was far too curious not to hear the man out.

"We can step around back to the patio." He gestured to the path that led around the side of the villa. Karl nodded and began walking around it. As the blades of grass brushed against his shoes, Eddy noticed his slightly off-kilter gait. He had never noticed it before. It wasn't as if he was drunk, it was more like he was favoring one foot over the other.

"Are you hurt, Karl?" Eddy paused beside him as he reached the patio.

"No. Well." Karl lifted his pant leg to reveal a stiff, white bandage around his ankle. "A little."

"What happened?" Eddy raised an eyebrow. He didn't recall Karl being hurt in any way in the robbery.

"When Derek, the robber, wants to get his point across, he has his ways." Karl shook his head. "I didn't want to do it, but I had no choice."

"Do what, Karl?" Eddy leveled his gaze on the man. He didn't want to miss any indication that Karl might be lying.

"I used to work at a prison, and when I worked there Derek would talk to me a lot. To be honest with you I ignored him for a long time. But he kept pushing. He was interested in some of the same things I was. So, we struck up conversations about it, and over time, he became less like an inmate to me, and more like a friend. I had no idea."

"Why don't you just tell me everything from the beginning, Karl? If you're in some kind of trouble, of course I'll do my best to help you."

"Well, the situation was that Derek was going to be released. I thought it was great for him, that he'd have a fresh start, and so on. Then one day I had a visit from this stranger, Charlie." He narrowed his eyes. "She came to my house. She knew who I was. She claimed to be Derek's friend. She told me that she wanted me to quit my job and take one at a local bank."

"She just showed up at your door and asked you to do this?" Eddy frowned. "That didn't strike you as odd?"

"Are you kidding me? Of course it did." He sighed and rubbed one hand across his cheek. "Her gun was pretty convincing. She told me that Derek would be the one doing all of the dirty work. All I had to do was make sure there weren't any complications and give them a little bit of information about the opening and closing routines of the bank, what days the most money was in the bank, that kind of thing." He closed his eyes. "I know it was wrong. I know it was. But I didn't have a choice. She told me I had two options. I could cooperate, or she would kill me. Kill my family."

"That's not much of a choice." Eddy feigned sympathy. He wanted to keep Karl talking, but he was still very skeptical.

"Exactly. So you know, I did what I had to do. I didn't like it. But I didn't have a choice."

"Uh huh." Eddy nodded. "I guess going to the police was out of the question?"

"I didn't think I should risk it." He frowned. He wrung his hands together tightly. "I mean, that's why I came to you. If I walked into the police station right now and tried to tell them this they would just lock me up. I was hoping that maybe you could help me."

Eddy narrowed his eyes. "How do you think I could help, Karl?"

"I don't know. I guess I thought you would take the time to listen, and then maybe get me hooked up with someone who will work out a deal for me." He squinted against the last of the evening light. "I know I'm not getting out of this. But I want someone to hear my side of the story. I didn't have a choice."

"And the man that took the fall? The man who was murdered? Did he have a choice?" Eddy positioned himself carefully between Karl and the exit of the patio. He didn't want Karl to suddenly bolt on him.

"I don't know anything about that," Karl said with a shocked look. "I had nothing to do with any murder."

"I don't believe you, Karl." Eddy believed that Karl must have some knowledge of the murder. "Someone was murdered because of this robbery."

"I don't know anything about that," he repeated. "But it doesn't surprise me. Charlie is ruthless."

"So, you're telling me that you don't know about the murder and you had to help with the robbery." Eddy tried not to sound too skeptical.

"It's not like I don't feel guilty enough about the robbery. Sometimes I can't stop thinking about what might have been avoided if I had just resisted the friendship with Derek. But really, I never stood a chance. He knew things about me. I think Charlie was telling him things about me, in order to win my friendship. Then once he had me, it was easy to access me when he was out. I guess really, all of this is my fault, but I don't know how to get out of it now."

"Well, if you go to the police they will arrest you, there's no question about that." Eddy hesitated. He knew he should call Detective Brunner and tell him about Karl's confession, but he was worried that he would just put all the blame on Karl and might not even pursue Derek and Charlie if there wasn't enough evidence to support Karl's story. In normal circumstances Eddy wouldn't have doubted Detective Brunner's ability to do his job, but these weren't normal circumstances. He knew there was someone on the inside leaking information to Derek and trying to make sure that the spotlight stayed off Derek. So he needed to ensure that he had enough evidence so that would not be a possibility and ensure the safety of Karl while he was in police custody.

"I know I have to pay for my part in all of this." Karl sniffled and blinked quickly. "I don't want to have to go to jail, but I know my life is already ruined. I just don't want to see anyone else get hurt."

"All right, well I think what you should do is lay low for tonight." It went against every fiber of Eddy's being to advise a confessed criminal not to turn himself in. But Eddy wanted to get inside Derek's house first. He wanted to make sure that he had evidence that the man was involved in the robbery before Karl turned himself in. That way no one could dismiss the case without investigating Derek, which would hopefully lead to Charlie and then they could all be arrested. "In the morning, I'll take you in to talk to a detective I know. Karl, you've gotten yourself into a bad situation, but you're doing the right thing by telling the truth now. That should make you look good to the detective."

"I guess." He nodded. "If I just keep my head down tonight, hopefully by the morning I'll be on the road to being an honest person again."

"Let's hope so." Eddy eyed the man with what

he hoped was sympathy. He didn't actually feel much sympathy for him at all. He watched as Karl started to step around him towards the road. He paused at the last minute and turned back to Eddy.

"Thank you." He met Eddy's eyes. "I mean that. I know it has to be a burden on you to know all of this."

Eddy's cheeks flushed with heat. The hardness in Karl's eyes was enough to make him wonder if Charlie was really the mastermind after all.

"Anything I can do to help." Eddy hoped that his words were convincing.

Karl stared at him for a moment longer, then nodded. He continued down the path back towards the road. Eddy turned and watched as Karl disappeared into the darkness. Karl had sent a clear message. He knew who Eddy was, and he knew where he lived. Eddy suddenly had the unsettling thought that maybe he had gotten that information from Terry Carlil. But he knew that there were many sources that he could have got the information from. Eddy pulled out his cell phone and called Samantha. He wanted to make sure that she knew what they were up against.

"Eddy, is it time already?" Samantha sounded sleepy. Eddy realized she must have been taking a nap in preparation for their covert adventure.

"No, it's not. But you won't believe who I just had a visit from."

"Who?"

"Karl."

"Karl Connell?" Samantha suddenly sounded wide awake. "What was he doing here?"

"He came to me to confess that he was involved in the robbery, but he claimed that Derek and Charlie threatened him and his family if he didn't help. He asked for help because he wants to turn himself in."

"Huh. Did you call Detective Brunner?"

"Not yet. I told him to lay low until tomorrow." Eddy didn't mention that he didn't trust Detective Brunner at this point to not interfere in the investigation. He didn't trust him not to alert his superior to Eddy's involvement either.

"Eddy, I don't think that was a good idea."

"Maybe not, but I want to get some solid proof that Derek was involved in this crime. If I don't we might have a serious problem on our hands."

"As if we don't already. I can't believe he showed up there. Did he admit to knowing anything about the murder?" Samantha asked.

"No, he said he had nothing to do with that and he knew nothing about it. He claimed that Charlie threatened his life and his family's lives if he didn't help with the robbery."

"Oh wow. So he's trying to claim that he had no choice?"

"Exactly."

"Hm. Well, I think the fact that a large chunk of his mortgage has been paid off recently indicates differently."

"I agree." Eddy frowned. "I'm not sure what to think about Karl to be honest. What I do know is that we need to get this crime solved and fast, before it blows up in our faces."

Chapter Twelve

Eddy was relieved when he met the others at Jo's. He had been trying to think of a good angle to use on Karl ever since his visit, but he had yet to come up with one. He wanted Karl to admit that he was involved in the crime, not just because of force. If he did that and they could get the other two for the robbery as well and find out who the murderer was there would be a nice, neat case for Detective Brunner to solve. Presuming that Detective Brunner wanted to solve the case. He walked up to Samantha and Walt who stood outside Jo's villa.

"Where's Jo?"

"She's on her way out." Samantha tilted her head towards the door.

"I heard you had a surprise visitor." Walt squinted at Eddy. "Do you think he was telling the truth?"

"I don't know. Maybe a version of it." Eddy

shrugged. "He claimed that he had been injured by Derek. I don't know though, something just feels very off."

"Well, I don't see any evidence of him turning down those cash payments to pay off his mortgage, so I'd venture to say that he wasn't just in fear of his life," Walt said. "His pockets were being very well lined."

"Ready?" Jo stepped out of the front door. Eddy had to tighten his lips to keep from audibly gasping. It always shocked him a little when he saw Jo in her work clothes. Skin tight, and always black, the clothing left nothing to the imagination. Eddy had to remind himself that he had no business imagining anything to begin with.

"Ready." Eddy nodded.

"How do you even carry any tools in that get up?" Walt openly surveyed Jo's outfit.

"Do you really want to know, Walt?" She smirked at him.

"No, actually nope not at all." Walt took a step

back. Samantha covered her mouth with her hand to hide her laughter.

"Let's take Walt's car." Samantha glanced at her watch. "By the time we get there, Derek should have left. Hopefully we can get in and out without him ever being the wiser."

Eddy nodded. "That would be for the best." He didn't point out that so far nothing else had gone very smoothly in their investigation.

The drive to Derek's house was fairly short. Eddy did his best not to leave any evidence of his presence in Walt's car. The man was very particular and would detect even a fingerprint with the naked eye, Eddy was sure of it. They parked a few houses down. Jo and Walt took a moment to review the plan that they had put together.

"I'll go in the window and let you in the back," Jo explained the plan to Eddy as they climbed out of the car.

"Remember, I'm going to text you if someone is approaching the house or if we see any lights turned on in the house." Samantha frowned as she looked at the two. "Just make sure that you're careful."

"Don't worry." Jo smiled at her. "We'll be in and out before you know it."

"My phone is on." Eddy patted his pocket. As they walked away from the car there was not much movement in the neighborhood. Everyone on the street slept peacefully with no idea that anyone was preparing to break into one of their homes, the home of a criminal. There was no car in the drive so they presumed that Derek was at work as expected. They walked around the side of the house to the window that Jo planned to make her entrance through.

Jo checked the window thoroughly. Then she slid a thin, silver tool between the windowsill and the bottom of the window. Eddy watched with fascination as she slid the tool very carefully back and forth.

"Why are you doing that?"

"Sh." She shot him a look of warning. "It's to

check for any alarm sensors."

"Oh."

Eddy watched as she slid the tool back out. She then reached up to the top of the window. She slid the tool between the glass and the frame of the window. With one swift movement she knocked the lock out of place. She placed her gloved hands on the glass surface of the window and eased it up. The window opened easily. Eddy was impressed. He had no idea it was so easy to break into a home. With the window open she gestured to him to be quiet. He nodded. She pointed to the back door, confirming that she would let him in the back door. He nodded again. There was no way he was climbing in the window.

Jo swung her body right through the window. Eddy was impressed, again. She didn't even flinch at the physical strain. He walked towards the back door. As he waited for her to open it he thought about what her life must have been like when she was an active thief. Sure it was wrong, but he could imagine the thrill. Being able to break into even the most secure buildings had to be a special kind of high for her. He was guilty of enjoying a few of his investigations a little too much because of the adrenaline that had pumped through his veins. He felt that again as he waited by the door. After another minute slid by he came to an unsettling realization. Jo was not going to the back door. She never had any intention of letting him into the house. She presumed that once she was inside Eddy wouldn't risk going in after her and she was right, he wouldn't risk it. He would certainly not be as discreet at entering the house as she was.

Eddy moved back to the window and peered through it. He could see her shadow moving through the house. He was tempted to bang on the window to get her attention. But he didn't want to risk alerting anyone to their presence. With each minute that passed by the more his fury built. He felt foolish for letting her get the upper hand. He was just about to find his own way in, when the back door swung open. Eddy braced himself for the risk that it might be Derek walking out the door. Instead, it was Jo. As soon as she was clear of the door, he confronted her.

"What were you thinking?"

"I told you I work alone." Jo shrugged.

"Jo, that's too big a risk." Eddy snarled at her. "Do you think that you don't matter? Is that it? Do you not realize that if something had happened to you it would have been my fault?"

Jo looked at him with wide eyes. "Eddy, just calm down, everything went fine."

"But it might not have." He glared at her. "You shouldn't be so reckless with your life, Jo. You have people who care about you, you know."

Jo blinked once as if she might not know what to say. Then she cleared her throat. "I'll try to remember that."

"Good. And next time, I'll be going in first." Eddy sighed.

"Sh!" She steered him further away from the house. As soon as they were far enough away she turned to face Eddy. "All that matters is the job was done."

"Was it? Did you find anything?"

"Of course." She held up a small camera to reveal a photo of what looked like a floorplan that had been crumpled up and then smoothed out. Eddy recognized it as a sketch of the layout of the bank and down the side it had opening and closing times. He was surprised that Derek had kept it. She scrolled to the next photo which was of black gloves that the robber most likely wore on the day of the robbery.

"There's no evidence from the murder?" Eddy asked.

"Nothing that I could find." Jo shook her head. "But hopefully these will make Detective Brunner investigate Derek's involvement."

"I bet they will." Eddy hoped that when he showed the photos to Detective Brunner it would convince him to investigate Derek, but he still didn't know how he was going to explain to the detective how he got the photos. They made their way towards the car. Walt jumped out of the car and opened the door for Jo.

"She got what we needed." Eddy smiled with pride.

"Great, now we can finally go to Detective Brunner, right?" Samantha met Eddy's eyes.

"Yes. Well, after one more thing." Eddy cringed.

"What?" Samantha and Walt both looked at Eddy with disbelief.

"You wanted proof, now you have it. What more do you want?" Walt frowned.

"I want the chance to find out where the rest of that money is. If we don't figure out where the money is it might be gone forever," he explained. "The moment we bring Detective Brunner into this, the moment that Derek is arrested, we lose all control. Derek and Karl could clam up and not give up Charlie. Or none of them may reveal where the rest of the money is." He didn't mention that he hoped in the process he might find evidence to prove who the murderer was.

"Eddy, I admire your determination, especially when it comes to the money, but you may not be able to get proof of everything." Walt started the engine of the car. "Is it really worth more risk for you to find it?"

"Yes. I think it is." Eddy paused a moment. "But we went into this as a team, so it's not just my choice. If the three of you think we should go to Detective Brunner now, then that's what we'll do."

"Listen, if this woman is as vicious as you describe, I think it's worth going the extra mile to make sure she ends up behind bars." Jo looked over at Eddy. "What's the point of going to all of this trouble if we're not going to get them all?"

"She makes a good point." Samantha nodded from the front seat. "I guess one more day won't hurt anything."

"Keeping that money from making criminals rich is enough reason for me." Walt smiled as he drove towards Sage Gardens.

Chapter Thirteen

Eddy found it hard to sleep. His mind kept returning to those moments when he did not know what was happening inside the house. He had been so worried about Jo that it had been impossible for him to focus properly. As he lay awake in bed he struggled to piece together what he knew. After Karl visited him he was fairly sure that Charlie was in charge of everything. However, she had a few loose ends in Karl and Derek. Would she really leave them dangling? Eddy doubted it.

He had the impression that Charlie was going to make short work of the men as soon as she felt safe enough to do so. If he didn't intervene the only one that would end up alive and with all of the money would be Charlie and there would still be an unsolved murder. It was hard for him not to get up and call Detective Brunner as he hated the idea of withholding what he believed was actual proof. But he felt like he didn't have much choice, waiting to try and bring them all down was really his only option. When the sun rose Eddy was still awake and restless. He decided it was time for him to speak to Derek about the robbery, maybe he would turn on Charlie. He called Samantha.

"Eddy, are you awake already?" She yawned into the phone. "I feel like we just got back."

"If you want to sleep go right ahead, but I'm going over to Derek's. Now that I know he is the bank robber I want to ask him a few questions."

"Do you really think that's wise?" Samantha sounded nervous.

"We'll just have to be careful. That is if you decide to go with me."

"Of course I'm going with you!" Samantha insisted. "You're not going alone. I need about twenty minutes."

"All right. I'll pick you up." Eddy was not as reluctant as he pretended to be. He enjoyed having Samantha along on the investigation. Eddy decided not to alert Walt or Jo. He would update them if they found anything.

As he headed to Samantha's to pick her up he recalled the way that Charlie had acted so confidently when she spoke to the two men she had worked with. The woman was not someone that would easily be caught. She was smart enough to pull off almost the perfect robbery and he suspected almost the perfect murder as well. He doubted that she was going to risk one of the two men working for her, turning on her. The chance for them to truly solve the crime was fading fast. Samantha seemed to understand the urgency as she hurried to the car. Once she was seated inside she barely had her seatbelt buckled before she started talking.

"I did some more digging last night. I couldn't sleep. I decided to try and find out if, and how, Charlie is tied to John Baker, the man who was killed. It turns out that they were a couple at one time."

"A couple?" Eddy glanced over at her.

"And from what I found I don't think he was

involved in the robbery, I think he was their fall guy."

"I guess the relationship didn't end well." He drove out of Sage Gardens.

"No, actually he had taken a restraining order out on her, and was filing a civil suit for harassment. Which is probably what made him the perfect target to take the fall for the bank robbery."

"Ouch, to think that she was once involved with someone and now it looks like she murdered him. She has to be cruel." Eddy steered the car down the street that led to Derek's house. Since they had used Walt's car the night before he hoped that they would not be noticed.

"Well, it seems like there was a lot of bad blood between the two. I guess she figured that she could kill two birds with one stone."

"Hopefully, we can prevent that from happening and she'll be punished. I think it's clear that she orchestrated the murder. I would be very surprised if she didn't pull the trigger herself."

"Clear to us, we just have to make sure that it's clear to Brunner," Samantha said. "Yes, I think we need proof."

Eddy parked the car a few houses away from Derek's house. He gritted his teeth. "If he's interested in proof that is."

"What are we going to do when he answers the door?"

"We're just going to knock and strike up a conversation. We'll see what happens from there."

"Okay." Samantha got out of her side of the car. She was already halfway up the walkway when Eddy caught up with her.

"Remember, we need to be as casual as possible." Eddy reached up and knocked firmly on the door. He waited a few moments. There was no sign of movement inside the house.

"Maybe he's not home?" Samantha raised an eyebrow.

"Maybe." Eddy knocked again. This time he hit the wood a little harder. When he did the door swung open about a foot.

"Oops. It wasn't locked?" Samantha took a slight step back.

"Maybe Charlie already got to him." Eddy frowned. "I better take a look. You wait here."

"Oh, no way, you're not going in there without me." Samantha stepped up beside him once more. Eddy frowned, but he didn't want to take the time to argue. He knew that if there was any chance that Charlie had left Derek alive, he would need medical attention fast. Eddy pushed the door all of the way open and stepped cautiously inside. The interior of the house was dim as the curtains were drawn. Eddy moved slowly through the house with Samantha right behind him.

There were a few piles of clothes and other mess throughout the hallway and the entrance of the bedroom. Derek was clearly not the tidy type. He also was not in the house as far as Eddy could see.

"He's not here." Eddy turned around and bumped right into Samantha. Samantha tried to step back, but her foot caught on a pile of dirty laundry. She stumbled and hit the wall hard. A picture that hung precariously on the wall crashed down and struck the floor.

"Yikes, that wasn't exactly stealthy." Samantha cringed.

"Don't worry he's not here."

"We should go, we don't know when they might be coming back." Samantha started towards the door.

"Wait."

"Eddy, we agreed not to break in."

"Well, we didn't actually break in. We walked in, but now that we're here, we might as well take a look around." He kicked over a pile of clothes and picked up a crumpled piece of paper. He opened it to see it was just a receipt for some groceries. Eddy threw it back down on the floor.

"Eddy, Jo's already looked around. We don't have any idea where Derek is, and we don't have any lookouts. I don't think this is a good idea."

Samantha grabbed him by the hand. "Let's go. I have a bad feeling."

Eddy looked at her for a moment. He was about to point out that bad feelings weren't a reason to abandon an investigation when her words sunk in. He knew she was right. It was too risky to do a full search.

"All right, let me just put the painting back," Eddy said.

"Okay quickly. Who knows when Derek will be back." Samantha started towards the painting. Eddy followed after her. Before she could get near it, Eddy tugged her sharply towards the wall.

"Eddy!" Samantha protested

Eddy clamped a hand down over her mouth and pulled her into the coat closet beside the front door.

"He's coming," he hissed in her ear. They both heard the slam of two car doors in the driveway. Eddy realized that maybe hiding in the coat closet wasn't the best idea, but that's where they were, and it was too late to make a different choice. The door to the house swung open. Two voices filled the front entrance.

"Why is the painting on the floor?"

"Maybe it just fell off the wall."

The first voice was Derek. Eddy was surprised to hear that the second voice belonged to Karl, the security guard.

"Paintings don't just fall off the wall." Derek sounded annoyed. "I think someone's been here."

"Do you think it's Charlie?"

Samantha leaned closer to the door to listen. Eddy pulled her back behind him.

"Sh. Not a word." Eddy pushed her towards the back of the closet. Even though he wasn't touching her chest, he could feel her heart pounding. Maybe it was his heart pounding, but he suspected it was hers. He could hear the commotion outside the door.

"No, if it was Charlie, we would be dead," Derek hissed. "I'm going to take a quick look around. Make sure no one is in here." Eddy and Samantha didn't dare move. They waited frozen on the spot in anticipation of Derek opening the closet door. They heard Derek's footsteps as he walked around the house.

"Must be long gone," Derek said. Eddy and Samantha relaxed slightly.

"Maybe no one was even here."

"Someone was here, I'm sure of it." Derek's voice raised. "Someone has been asking the police about the case. Someone is onto us. I can feel it. If Charlie gets wind of it, she's going to panic, that's why we need to figure out what to do."

"What do you mean?" Karl sounded frightened. "I'm not doing anything to upset Charlie."

"I'm not doing anything to upset Charlie," Derek repeated in a mocking tone. "Do you think that woman would hesitate to kill you, Karl? You're the weakest link out of all of us."

"That's not fair. I did my part."

"You almost got us caught in the process." Derek snarled. Eddy wondered if he was talking about the robbery or murder.

"Does Charlie know that?"

"It doesn't matter what Charlie knows. The only thing you should worry about is who else knows? Have you told anyone anything, Karl? Because somehow someone is looking into us. If it was the cops, then we would be in handcuffs. Cops don't break into houses, they get warrants."

"Uh well."

Eddy cringed inside the closet. He hoped that Karl wasn't going to tell Derek about his meeting with Eddy. If he did then Eddy would be even more of a target than he already was. Which would make finding him and Samantha in the closet even more dangerous. Would Derek hesitate to kill them both? He felt Samantha's hand slide into his own. Normally it would inspire awkward feelings within him, but at that moment, he was relieved to feel it.

"Uh, well what?" Derek shouted. "Who did

you tell, Karl?"

"I didn't tell anyone, exactly."

"Answer the damn question. Don't play word games with me." Derek sounded as if he was about to explode.

"Look, I needed to protect myself, my family. You know, I'm not a criminal."

"You are now," Derek snapped. "You're just as much a criminal as the rest of us. You agreed to be part of this."

Eddy narrowed his eyes. He had suspected that Karl lied about being forced to be part of the robbery. Karl was quite manipulative as well. It appeared that he tried to play the victim when he was willingly involved the entire time.

"Whatever. I have a lot more to lose. I don't want to go to prison. I wouldn't do well there."

"You sure wouldn't. So you better keep your mouth shut. Who did you tell? I'll take care of it."

"No wait..."

Eddy heard the door swing open, and the two

men fell instantly silent.

"Karl, what are you doing here?" Eddy froze as he recognized the voice. Charlie. There was no way they were getting out of there with Charlie just outside the door.

"We're just having a conversation, Charlie." Derek sounded nervous.

"A conversation without me? About me?" Charlie's voice raised. "Do you know how this looks to me?" She slammed the door closed behind her.

"It's not what you think." Karl sounded terrified. "Charlie, we're just sorting out a few things."

"You shouldn't be sorting anything out without talking to me first. Get away from the door. Get into the living room, away from the windows."

"Why?" Karl questioned with a trembling voice. "Why do we have to be away from the windows?"

"Why? Because I told you to. I don't want anyone spotting the three of us together. I'm already annoyed that I have to be here right now. If you two idiots didn't keep messing things up, everything would be fine, and we wouldn't even have to look at each other."

Eddy heard footsteps as the three shuffled past the closet. He was relieved that there would now be some distance between them. He thought about edging the closet door open. They could attempt to run out the door before they were seen. However, he knew that would be taking a huge risk. The three were still talking loudly enough for Eddy and Samantha to hear them.

"Why don't you two start telling me the truth?" Charlie's voice smoothed out. Her confidence had built up again. "There's no way either of you are leaving this room without telling me."

"All right, all right." Karl cleared his throat. "I'm meeting with Derek because I wanted to know about the money."

"The money? What money?" Charlie snarled.

"Look, you said when the job was done we'd split the money. Now we've given some of that money to the cops. I want to know where the rest of that money is." Karl's voice tried to get stronger, but it didn't have the confidence to make it. Eddy knew that Karl was talking about the money the police found with John. He wanted to try and record the conversation in case Charlie admitted to the murder, but he didn't dare move.

"You want to know? Rent-a-cop? You're the only one out of all of us that saw some real cash, so what are you complaining about?"

"It's not just him," Derek broke in, his voice was rough. "I want my share, too. We did everything you asked, we want our money now. I want out of all of this before the heat kicks in."

"There will be no heat." Charlie sighed. "Listen boys, you're falling for it. This is what ruins a great heist. Dissent. Panic. Idiocy. We need to wait, just a little while longer. A few more days and the robbery will be a distant memory.

Then you'll get your money and we can all move on."

"That's easy for you to say." Derek's voice raised. "You have all of the money."

"I don't have it. I know where it is. I can access it," she said.

"I want to see it. How do I know that you even have it? You could have spent it all. Your dead ex-boyfriend might have had the only cash that was left," Derek sounded furious as he spat out his words.

"You're out of control, Derek. Do I need to remind you of exactly who I am?"

"No, no. I'm sorry." Derek's tone shifted so fast that Eddy was shocked. It made him wonder just who this woman was that she could make a man like Derek submit to her so easily. "I'm just getting anxious. You know there's been these people sniffing around. I think someone was in my house."

"Derek, you're just getting paranoid. Stay

inside, keep your head down, don't worry about anyone sniffing around. We're almost out of the danger zone. Then we'll all be living the good life. Just keep your cool a little bit longer. Understand?"

"Yeah, I understand," Derek muttered.

"Karl?" Charlie's voice was sharp.

"Yes, I understand." Karl sounded spooked.

"All right. I don't want to even think about the two of you trying to do anything to cause me any trouble. I promise you, if I get the slightest bit anxious about my decision to trust you two, I'm going to make you pay the price."

Silence followed her harsh words, until the front door slammed shut indicating that she had left. Eddy knew that he had to get Samantha out of there before the two men discovered them. He reached for the door knob. When he heard the two men begin to talk again, he froze.

"She's crazy. You know that don't you?" Karl's voice was filled with urgency.

"Karl, just calm down."

"I'm not going to calm down. I know what's going to happen. Either you two are going to set me up to take the fall, or I'm going to end up hurt or worse. I'm not the idiot that you think I am, Derek."

"You're acting like one right now. You heard Charlie, she's being smart about things. You're the one who's about to mess everything up. Now, who did you talk to about the robbery?"

Eddy looked over his shoulder at Samantha. He knew there was only one way he could protect her.

"Stay here," he whispered. "No matter what." He met her eyes through the shadows, inside the closet. "I mean it, Samantha."

"What are you going to do, Eddy?" Her eyes widened with fear.

"Never mind, just keep quiet and stay here until I say it's safe." He gazed into her eyes with a hard stare. "Please."

"I will." Samantha nodded. Eddy turned back towards the door. He could hear Karl and Derek still arguing in the living room. He turned the knob on the door and stepped out. Then he quickly closed the door behind him.

"He talked to me, that's who he talked to."

Both men looked at him in shock.

"I knew it, I knew someone had broken into my house!" Derek snarled. "Who the hell are you?"

"I'm nobody," Eddy started to explain, but before he could Derek had him slammed back against the closet door.

"Wait, Derek don't, he's a cop. Or at least he used to be," Karl gasped.

Derek's eyes widened. "What is going on here?" He looked from Karl to Eddy and then back to Karl. "Why would you talk to a cop about us?"

"I'm not a cop. Not anymore." Eddy looked between them. "That's why he talked to me. He knew that I could help him."

"Help him with what?" Derek's cheeks were bright red. His eyes squinted with rage as he looked at Karl.

"Like I said, I was expecting you and Charlie to double-cross me. I thought Eddy could give me some advice about how to navigate a plea deal." Karl took a step back. "But I didn't go through with it, Derek, did I? I'm here aren't I?"

"Is this some kind of set up?" Derek demanded.

"No, not at all." Eddy frowned. "I want a cut." It was hard for him to even speak those words, but he knew the only way to get out of the situation was to lie. "After Karl came to me and told me that he had been involved, I thought about it, and decided I wanted in on the action. I'm retired now and money is tight. So, I want some cash in exchange for my silence and my advice."

"Why would I ever need advice from you?" Derek shook his head. "This is ridiculous. Charlie was right, I should have gotten rid of you." He scowled at Karl.

"Sure, you seem to have everything under control. At least until Charlie decides that she doesn't want to share that money. Boys, if we play our cards right, you won't have to share it with her. I have enough proof now to put her away for a long time, but first we need to find out where the money is. Otherwise she'll be in jail and we'll all still be broke."

Eddy's stomach twisted. He knew that he was taking a huge chance.

"Listen to him, Derek. Do you really think Charlie is going to give us our share?" Karl shook his head. "I never thought you'd want a cut, but if that's what you want, Eddy, you'll get it. What's your plan for getting the money?"

"Quiet!" Derek slammed his hands against his temples. "Everything is changing too fast. Why should I let you in on the deal?"

"Because you're not going to be rich without my help. You're just going to be dead. If you let me in on the money, then I can make sure that you get everything you want. I will keep you out of jail, and together we can pin everything on Charlie. Then she doesn't kill you, doesn't get any of the money, and will be the only one paying the price."

"You can't really do all of that." Derek shook his head. "I don't believe it."

"No?" Eddy smiled. "I got in here didn't I? Without you knowing? I know that the man that was murdered was Charlie's ex. She should have known better than to bring personal stuff into all of this. They are eventually going to make the connection between the murdered man and her, and then the police will have every reason to suspect her."

"He has a point." Karl frowned. "She wants to spin all of this around on us, but she's not expecting us to do the same. I think she's ready to get rid of both of us. So, what's the difference if we share the money with Charlie or with Eddy? At least we might stay alive." Karl shrugged. "I think we should go for it."

"And how exactly are we going to do that?" Derek scowled. "It's not like Charlie is just going to tell us where the money is."

"Don't worry about that. I can find the money." Eddy smirked. "I have a guy."

"Oh?" Derek shook his head. "I guess you're ready to trade in your life of justice for a life of crime."

"Crime pays better." Eddy shrugged.

"Hm." Derek studied him intently. "How do I know you won't cross us?"

"You don't. Just like you don't know if Charlie will. The difference is I don't have an ego that needs to be stroked. I don't have any reason to take you out of the equation. I just want some cash, just like the two of you." Eddy did his best to sound convincing. It wasn't completely untrue. A financial windfall would be very nice for him. But he would never become a criminal to get it.

"I don't know." Derek shook his head. "All of this seems too strange."

"Stranger than trusting a woman who keeps threatening our lives?" Karl shook his head. "I think we should just talk it through. See what Eddy has to offer us."

"Let's do that." Derek nodded.

"How about that little coffee shop where you and Charlie met yesterday?" Eddy smiled. "I know all about that meeting."

"How?" Derek's eyes widened.

"Like I said, I have information on all of you. I don't want to send you to jail. I just want a cut. So, let's go have some lunch boys."

"All right." Karl nodded. "Derek?"

"I could eat." Derek sighed.

Eddy knew that as soon as he had them out of the house Samantha would be able to escape. What he didn't know was how he was going to convince two criminals that he was a criminal just like them.

Chapter Fourteen

The ride to the coffee shop in Derek's car was nerve-wracking. Eddy's heart pounded the entire time. He wondered if Samantha had managed to get out of the closet. He didn't dare call her. He didn't want to do anything to tip off the men that he was riding with that he had not been honest with them. Derek parked in front of the coffee shop.

"I think this was a bad idea. What if Charlie sees us? She's always here." Karl frowned.

"So, what if she does? Let her sweat it out a bit." Derek smirked.

Eddy saw his chance to escape. "All right look, there's no need to antagonize her. Why don't I go see my guy about finding out where the money is? You two can hash out whatever you need to hash out. We can meet back at Derek's tomorrow morning to discuss things."

"That's awful fast," Derek said. "Why are you

rushing things?"

"Do you want to wait for Charlie to pick you off one by one so she can keep all of the money?" Eddy laughed. "I thought you were smarter than that, Derek."

"All right, all right. We'll meet at my place tomorrow morning. No funny business."

"Do you need us to take you somewhere?" Karl offered. Eddy was reminded that he still had an honorable nature.

"No, that's all right, I can find my way." He opened the door and stepped out. Just when he thought he was in the clear, Derek called out to him.

"Eddy wait."

Eddy turned back slowly. He looked into the eyes of the man who he presumed was concealing a gun. "What?"

"Don't make me regret this. No more breaking into my house, understand?"

"I understand." Eddy nodded. His heart

flipped. Derek nodded as well and started the engine of the car. As Eddy watched them drive away he pulled out his cell phone. He quickly called Samantha.

"Eddy? Are you okay? I was afraid to call!" Samantha sounded like she was in a panic.

"I'm fine, I promise. Are you out of the house?"

"Yes, I'm by your car."

"Okay, if you look in the glove compartment you'll find a spare key." Eddy gave her instructions of where it was. "Drive over to the coffee shop where we watched Charlie and pick me up."

"Eddy, are you sure you're okay?"

"I promise, Samantha, but I'll be a lot better when I put some distance between myself and this place. Okay?"

"I'll be there in five minutes." Samantha hung up the phone. Eddy was so glad she was safe. Now, he had to figure out what kind of mess he had just gotten himself into. Sure, he and Samantha were safe, but he had two criminals who expected him to help them double-cross a ruthless criminal. He might have talked himself into a situation he couldn't get out of. He dialed another number on his cell phone.

"Walt! It's Eddy. I think I'm going to need your help."

Samantha pulled up just as Eddy hung up the phone with Walt. Eddy opened the door to take over driving and Samantha practically flew out of the car at him.

"What were you thinking? I heard what you said to those men. If you don't do what you said you would, they are going to come after you, Eddy. How could you do that?" She glared at him.

"Calm down, Sam, let's just get out of here." He slid in behind the steering wheel. "Hurry."

Samantha scowled, but ran around the car to the passenger side. She fumed as Eddy pulled out of the parking lot.

"I didn't know what else to do." Eddy frowned. "It's not like I had a lot of options."

"I know." Samantha sighed. "I know that you did what you did to protect me, Eddy, I'm not stupid. I just wish you hadn't promised to work with them."

"Well, that's where we're at." He shook his head. "I wouldn't say it was my best moment, either."

"So, what are you going to do about it?" Samantha gripped the side of her seat. "What do you think they're going to do when you don't show up for the meeting tomorrow? Are you going to go to Detective Brunner now, Eddy? This has gone on long enough. We have the information we need to at least get Karl and Derek arrested."

"Right, but unless they provide credible enough proof of Charlie's involvement, she's going to get off scot-free. Then what? We failed completely at what we tried to do. We don't even have proof of who murdered John. I don't think it's time to go to the police yet." Eddy turned into

Sage Gardens.

"Are you kidding me?" Samantha glared at him. "We have to go to the police. Derek and Karl might come after you. Let's not forget that Karl knows where you live, Eddy. You have to tell Detective Brunner today, or I will."

Eddy stopped the car in Walt's driveway. He looked over at Samantha. "You'll do no such thing."

"Eddy, I can do whatever I please. If I want to go to Detective Brunner with what I've found then that is what I will do." She narrowed her eyes.

"Great, then you might as well just put the handcuffs on me right now." He held out his hands with his palms facing down. "Go ahead and lock me up because that's what is going to happen when Detective Brunner goes to question two bank robbers and they tell him that I am involved in the crime as well."

"Eddy, you're not really involved." Samantha frowned. "Detective Brunner will know that."

"In case you don't remember Brunner isn't the one who is running the show over there. That honor goes to someone who is connected to Derek. Don't you think that same someone could very easily decide to use me as a scapegoat instead?" Eddy opened his car door. "No, we're just going to have to see this thing through. I'm trusting you, Samantha, not to go to Detective Brunner until I say it's time. At this point, I'm not convinced he isn't involved somehow. He might even be the person feeding information to Derek."

"Detective Brunner?" Samantha shook her head. "Eddy, that's crazy. And I thought you said we were a team." Samantha got out of the car as well and blocked his way towards Walt's front door. "You said we were all in this together, so all of our opinions should matter. This idea that you have that you can just do whatever you please, put yourself at whatever risk you choose, that's the problem that we're having. Because you can't just throw yourself to the wolves, Eddy."

"I'm trying not to." Eddy winced. "I know

what I did was reckless. I couldn't think of anything better to do at the time. Now, the only way I'm going to get out of it is if we can actually find that money. If we find the money then we will be ready to go to Brunner. He will have enough proof that no matter what anyone tries to do on the inside, the proof will speak for itself. Really, it's the only way to make sure that we're all safe."

"I don't know, Eddy. You know I'm not the first one to run to the police, but this is getting a little out of control." Samantha frowned. "You know it's not because I don't trust you. It's because I don't want to see you get hurt."

"I know and I am the one that brought us all into this." Eddy sighed. "Don't think that I don't regret it. Some birthday gift."

"It's a great gift. I just don't want to see anyone else get hurt because of it." The front door of Walt's villa opened and Walt stepped out onto the porch.

"Eddy? Samantha? Are you coming in?"

"We'll be right there." Samantha nodded.

"Eddy, just remember that you're not the only one who wants to solve this, and you shouldn't be the only one that is taking the risk."

"I hear you, Samantha." Eddy nodded. He looked up at Walt. "Ready to do some real digging?"

"I'm ready." Walt nodded.

"Anything I can do to help?" Jo stepped out of the house behind Walt.

"Well, I guess the crew is all here." Eddy offered a nervous laugh. "Let's get inside and discuss this."

They all gathered around Walt's desk.

"So, what I need you to do is figure out where the money is!" Eddy explained.

"Oh, that's all?" Walt peered up at him. "You want me to figure out where a criminal has hidden thousands of dollars. From what?"

"I don't know, just see what you can find, previous crimes, places she frequents."

"I'll do my best." Walt frowned. "I'm not sure

that I will be able to find anything though."

"Just see what you can find."

"I can't believe you got yourself involved in a bank robbery." Jo shook her head and smiled with admiration. "I think that you are better at being a criminal than you would like to admit."

"Maybe I am. All I know is I don't want this woman getting away with the robbery or the murder."

"Here, I just found a picture of Charlie from a few years ago." Samantha showed Eddy the picture on her phone. "She looks like she's living the good life."

"Wait, is that Charlie?" Jo stared at the screen of Samantha's phone.

"Yes." Samantha looked up at Jo. "Why? Do you recognize her?"

"Uh yeah, I do." Jo glanced up at Eddy for a moment and then back down at the phone. "She must have changed her name, but she's pretty well-known in the robbery circles. She's pulled off quite a few large heists."

"So, this isn't her first time." Eddy smirked. "That's why she was able to come up with something so complicated to cover her tracks."

"Yes, and she was also known for her ruthlessness, she has no problem getting blood on her hands. She would leave guards, witnesses, sometimes just bystanders in her wake, either dead or close enough." Jo shook her head. "It's disgusting. There's never a reason that murder has to be involved with theft."

"That pretty much confirms it. She has mixed the two again. I'm almost sure that she pulled the trigger and murdered her ex," Eddy said. "Now I need the proof."

"This woman is dangerous. I'm not so sure it's wise to keep getting involved in all of this with her. I think maybe it's time to turn things over to the police," Jo said.

"We can't do that." Eddy shook his head firmly. "I'm not throwing away the entire investigation over one woman."

"She's not just one woman." Jo's eyes flashed as she argued. "She's a horrible person that will stop at nothing to make sure that anyone who crosses her suffers. Eddy, you don't know what you're dealing with."

"So, tell me. If you know her so well, then tell me." He looked at Jo. "What can I expect?"

"That's just the thing, she is unpredictable. The only thing you can know for sure is that she will do anything to get what she wants." Jo frowned.

"What about her previous heists?" Eddy's eyes widened. "Did you ever hear of where she would store her cash?"

"Hm." Jo closed her eyes for a moment. "I never heard of any specific place, but I can tell you that anyone who pulls off that large of a heist is going to put the money in a safe place, but a close place. She will want to be close enough to it to go check on it, to keep an eye on it."

"That doesn't seem like a smart move," Eddy said.

"It doesn't, but if you've worked that hard to steal a fortune, you're going to want to keep it close to you," Jo said. "It's common not to spend it or move it much in the days after it's stolen as that will alert the police. But keeping it close is the traditional thing to do."

"You said she would keep it close, like in her house?" Walt asked without looking away from the computer screen.

"No, not in her house. She would never risk that. Plus, she wouldn't want her accomplices to know where the money was. Just in case they tried to double-cross her. So, it wouldn't be in the house, but it would be somewhere nearby."

"What kind of distance are we talking?" Walt started typing on the keyboard.

"I don't know, probably no more than ten or fifteen miles away. Sometimes they use storage facilities, or even an underground bunker, things like that."

"Okay. That helps." Walt continued typing on the computer.

"I just think this is asking for trouble. What are we going to do if we find the money? You're not really going to tell them where it is, are you, Eddy?" Samantha questioned.

"Well, it would be a good way to get all three of them." Eddy nodded his head towards the computer screen. "I can tell Karl and Derek to go there and tip off Charlie that they're going. If they all end up at the same place where the money is then the police can arrest all of them. I don't know how I'm going to prove Charlie's responsible for the murder without a confession, though."

"If Charlie thinks they're going to get her money she will do whatever it takes to stop them." Jo nodded.

"Wait, I think I might have it." Walt sounded as surprised as Eddy felt. "I think I found the money."

"Really? Where is it?" Eddy leaned over him to have a closer look.

"When Jo said that Charlie would keep the money somewhere nearby, somewhere familiar, I started by looking into the coffee shop which she regularly frequents. There wasn't anything there to find. I then looked at a five mile radius from Charlie's home and I found a new storage facility. The storage facility is right behind the coffee shop."

"So, you think that Charlie hid the money there?" Eddy nodded.

"I think it's the best place to start looking," Walt replied. "It fits all the criteria."

"That makes sense. She's close enough to keep an eye on it," Eddy agreed.

"Well, it's worth looking into. I'll call the facility and see if they can give me any information," Samantha offered.

The three friends waited in silence as Samantha made the phone call.

"Bingo!" Samantha announced when she got off the phone. "She rented a locker in her name."

"That must be the place. But why would she rent it under her name? That's a little sloppy don't you think?" Eddy said.

"I do." Walt looked troubled. "But people do make mistakes. I guess this was hers."

"Maybe you have to show identification to rent the locker," Samantha suggested.

"Or she might have felt so confident that she wouldn't get caught that she didn't feel the need to be cautious." Jo shrugged. "It happens to the most seasoned thieves."

Eddy arched an eyebrow, but he kept his mouth shut. His mind churned with the next steps in his plan.

"And get this, the guard also said that she had a safe delivered to the storage locker," Samantha said.

"How did you get the information?" Eddy asked with admiration.

"I bent the truth a bit to get the information on the locker and he just told me about the safe," she shrugged. "He said he thought it was strange."

"Good work, Samantha." Jo smiled.

"If I let Derek and Karl know that I know about the locker, they're going to go there together to try to get the money. Then we'll have them, and the money, in the same place." Eddy frowned. "Then I'll find a way to get Charlie there."

"So, you're going to meet them tomorrow morning and tell them about this?" Samantha asked.

"Yes, I think that's the best way to do it." Eddy looked over at Samantha. "I want to make sure that we can all feel safe when all of this is over."

"Well, I'm afraid I don't agree with that." Walt pushed back from his desk. "I think it's a terrible idea."

"Why?" Eddy was surprised. "It's the best way to make sure that the money is recovered and they are arrested and then maybe the police will investigate them for the murder and find out exactly who is responsible."

"You're talking about tipping off two criminals that you know where the money from a bank robbery is being held. But you're not thinking about what they are going to do to you if they think that you are a threat to their cash and their freedom. So, what happens once you tell Derek and Karl you know where the money is? Then you tip off Charlie? Then they all decide to take you out, since you're on to them." Walt looked at Eddy. "You know as well as I do that they will come prepared to do whatever it takes. How do you plan on not getting caught in the crossfire?"

"Walt, I know how to protect myself. I'll be prepared."

"Or we could just go to Detective Brunner with what we have." Samantha crossed her arms. "I'm sure that he will help us if we explain the entire situation to him."

Eddy sighed and ran his hands across his cheeks. "Look, if we go to Brunner it's going to be a bad situation. If he is involved with all of this, if they've paid him off, then he will either have me arrested or let them kill me."

"Eddy, you don't know that Detective Brunner is part of this. He's never given you reason to doubt him before. Maybe he just doesn't think it's worth looking so closely at the case. None of us are police officers and we need the police involved."

Walt stood up and crossed his arms. "You're not alone in this situation. If we all think that it would be best to call the police, then that is what we should do. Am I right? Jo? Samantha?" He looked between the two women.

"I think so." Samantha nodded. She couldn't look directly at Eddy.

"I agree." Jo lifted her chin. "Even if you don't get Charlie, we'll get ourselves out of this situation."

"I can't just leave this alone. I can't risk Charlie getting away with it," Eddy said with determination.

"All right, that's up to you. You guys figure out what to do. Just leave my name out of it," Jo said.

"We will," Eddy assured Jo before she turned and walked out of the villa.

"Okay, let's sort this out and get in contact with Detective Brunner." Walt picked up his phone.

"Wait, wait! Let's just think this through. Why don't we table it for today? In the morning I'll go down to the police station and speak to Brunner myself. That's the best way to make sure that the information gets into the right hands." Eddy started to walk towards the door. "So, that's what we'll do, all right?"

"That sounds fair." Walt nodded. "I'm glad we'll at least be able to tell them where the money is."

Eddy nodded and managed a smile. He still wasn't convinced that Brunner wasn't Derek's contact. He decided not to mention that the police wouldn't be able to search for the money without a warrant, and wouldn't be able to get a warrant without some solid evidence that it was at the storage facility. Eddy walked out of the villa with his frustration building. He knew that everything he had tried to do was going to go to waste the moment that he spoke to Detective Brunner. That was why he couldn't speak to him. Eddy was almost to his car when Samantha caught up to him.

"Eddy wait."

"What is it, Samantha?"

"Are you okay?"

"I'm fine," he replied. "I just really want to get home and rest a little."

"I know you're disappointed with how this is ending, Eddy. I just want you to know that you can talk to me if you want to." She reached out and took his hand in hers. "We're friends, Eddy, you can tell me what you're feeling."

"I know that, Sam. I really appreciate it, but I'm fine. You are all right. It was too much of a risk to take, and it needs to be settled. I just want to make sure I can't think of another way before I talk to Brunner. All right?" He managed a smile.

Samantha stared at him as if she was searching for something.

"Are you sure that you're okay?"

"I'm sure." Eddy turned towards his car. He was surprised when he felt her hand on his arm.

"Eddy, promise me that you will not do anything by yourself." Samantha looked at him pleadingly. "I know that you want this case solved, but this is the best way to do it. I just want you to know that all the hard work you did was not for nothing. Two criminals are going to be behind bars, and that's much better than none. Don't you think?"

"Of course. Yes, it's better, Sam," he reluctantly agreed. "I just got too caught up in my old ways. I wanted to get to the core of it, and even when I was a detective that wasn't always possible. I'll be fine, I just need to be with my own thoughts for a bit. Okay?"

"You're sure you don't want company?" She met his eyes.

"I'm sure. Not today, Sam. But thank you." Eddy opened the door to his car. "I will let you know when I speak to Brunner."

"Do you want me to come with you to talk to him?" Samantha perked up as if she looked forward to it.

"I don't think so. It's better if it's just me. If anything doesn't go as planned, I don't want your name involved in the investigation. Bye Sam." He leaned over and gave her a light hug. Samantha stiffened and then smiled.

"Bye Eddy. Have a good night. Or at least try to."

"Okay." He smiled.

As Eddy drove away he looked in the rearview mirror. He hoped that this wasn't the last time he would see Samantha, but his decision had already been made.

Chapter Fifteen

As Eddy was driving the short distance to his villa he was thinking about the decision he had made. He felt comfortable with it even though he wasn't completely sure if it was the right one. All of a sudden something strange caught his attention. Outside Paul Carlil's house was Terry's car. There was nothing strange about the car being there she was his granddaughter after all, but what was strange was the fact that Paul was standing in the doorway of his villa talking to someone. Eddy recognized straight away that it was Karl.

Eddy slowed down, he was about to pull over on the side of the road and jump into action to protect Paul when the men shook hands and Paul ushered Karl inside. They seemed friendly with each other. Eddy didn't know what to make of the situation, but he decided that he needed to find out what was going on. He continued to his villa and parked his car there then he swiftly walked back to Paul's place. Eddy was almost at the door when it swung open in front of him. He quickly moved to the side of the house and hid in the shadows. Terry, Karl and Paul stood in the doorway.

"Thanks, Grandad," Terry said as she kissed him on the cheek.

"See you soon, Paul." Karl shook the man's hand.

Eddy's heart was pounding. He couldn't believe he had doubted his initial instincts. Terry was involved all along.

Terry and Karl walked towards Terry's car. Eddy was ready to confront them both, he wanted to find out the truth. Eddy expected to hear them talk about how they had pulled off the robbery, how they had succeeded and fooled everyone, instead Terry started crying.

"Please, Karl," she said in a low, trembling voice. "Please just leave him alone."

"I told you, Terry," he said gently. "You have

nothing to worry about from me. You've done your part. You will be okay. You just need to keep your mouth shut now."

"So, what are you doing here?" she asked. "I thought you were going to leave him alone."

"I just wanted one last visit to say goodbye." Karl shrugged and then looked into her eyes with a stern expression. "And to remind you of the consequences if you don't keep quiet."

"I never told anyone." She sounded genuinely upset to Eddy. Could she have been pulled into this?

"Just keep it that way and you'll be fine," Karl warned.

"I'm so scared," Terry said through her tears. "What about the others? What if they come after me? After Grandad?"

"They won't," he said. "They don't care about you, you're nothing to them. They know that you're taken care of."

"I wish I'd never gotten into this."

"I'm sorry. Just keep quiet and you'll be fine." With that he turned on his heel and walked towards the street where Eddy presumed his car was parked.

Terry steadied herself against the car. Eddy knew that he could be booked for stalking or harassment if he tried to talk to Terry again. She had made it clear that she had no issue calling the police. But he needed to find out the truth. She seemed scared and he needed to know how she was involved.

Eddy knew that if he confronted her then and there she would probably scream or at least he would scare the life out of her. Then the police would be called and he might never find out the truth.

Eddy waited until Terry got in her car and then he ran to his. He wished he could get Samantha to come with him to talk to her, but that wasn't an option. It was too late now. He quickly caught up to her, but he kept his distance so she wouldn't spot his car. Eddy recognized that they were heading to her house. As he followed Terry his heart pounded. He tried to piece together everything he had overheard. Terry was obviously involved somehow, but it didn't seem willingly.

As Eddy pulled up to Terry's house she was getting out of the car. He quickly got out of his, he had to get to her before she got into her house otherwise the opportunity would be lost.

Eddy parked the car and walked straight up to her.

"I don't want to hurt you," he said as she looked at him trying to process what was happening. "I want to help you."

"You again," she said. "Get away from me, you crazy man."

"Terry," Eddy said gently. "I just want to help you. I overheard you talking to Karl and I know that you are involved in all of this. I can help you."

"No one can help me."

"I can help," Eddy repeated. "You just need to tell me the truth and we can put them all behind bars. You won't have to be scared anymore."

"I should have kept quiet in the first place and then I wouldn't be in this position."

"What position?" Eddy said trying to get the truth out of her.

"It doesn't matter now." She shook her head. "I just tried to do what was right and now it's all a mess."

"Tell me what happened," he said. "I know you didn't have anything to do with the robbery. Just tell me the truth."

"Okay," she said hesitantly "But out here. I'm not letting you in my house I don't trust anyone anymore." She walked Eddy up to her porch and they sat down across from each other at a table.

"I had no idea what was going on until the robbery," she said as she took a tissue out of her purse.

"What was going on?" Eddy asked wishing Samantha was there. He knew that she would get to the truth faster.

"When Karl started working at the bank I was immediately suspicious of him. He seemed so interested in the workings of the bank." She wiped her eyes with the tissue. "You know procedures and other things that had nothing to do with him. I told him somethings at first and we went out for coffee a few times. He seemed so intent on befriending me. I thought maybe he just liked me. But then the robbery happened and I saw the way he acted and everything came together."

"You worked out he was involved," he pressed gently. He didn't want her to clam up. From her body language and what he had overheard her say to Karl, Eddy knew she was telling the truth.

"I suspected it," she said. "But I never wanted to believe it. But after the robbery I ran after him to ask him about it and he denied everything. And then…" she started crying.

"It's okay," Eddy said. "Take your time." He had heard Samantha say that to upset people that she wanted to get information from, but what he really wanted to say was, hurry up.

"Then I received some photos from him. He was with my grandfather. He had become his friend. I couldn't believe it. He said that if I did anything my grandfather would get it."

"He blackmailed you?" Eddy's eyes widened.

"I didn't know what to do." She grimaced. "I was so scared and then you came to see me and I had to get you off my back so I called the police. I couldn't let Karl think I would tell anyone about him, including you. I'm sorry."

"It's okay."

"I don't know what to do," she said. "I haven't told my grandfather because I don't want him to worry, but I'm scared."

"It's okay," Eddy said again with more determination. "I will protect you and the way I'm going to do that is by getting these criminals arrested."

"What if they come after me?"

"Don't worry I'll make sure your name is kept out of it." Eddy didn't like that Terry had kept information from him and the police, but he understood it. She was one of the people that needed protecting not punishing.

"How?"

"You don't need to worry about that," he said. "You just take care of yourself and get some rest. This will be over very soon."

She nodded her head as she stood up and walked towards her door. When she had stepped just inside the door she turned around. "I hope you're right," she said before she closed the door.

Eddy hoped that he was right, too. He was more determined than ever to make sure that these criminals were put behind bars not just for the crimes they had committed, but to protect Terry and Paul, the innocent members of the community. He walked to his car and slowly drove back to Sage Gardens. He wanted to call Samantha to tell her about the conversation he had just had with Terry, but it was late and he didn't want to wake her or have her worrying about it. She would find out soon enough. One thing was becoming clear to Eddy, Karl was guilty of more than being an accomplice to a robbery. If Karl was responsible for blackmail was he also responsible for murdering John?

Chapter Sixteen

When Eddy woke up the next morning he felt as if he had the best night's sleep ever. He felt comfortable with the choice he had made. Even if this was the last action he took in his life, he was satisfied, because he would be doing what he loved, serving justice. He straightened his hat and grabbed his old, small tape recorder and placed it in his pocket. He might be able to use it to record their confessions to the robbery, the more proof the better. He found the recorder on his phone much too difficult to handle secretively or when he was in a rush.

When Eddy made it to the car he felt his heart begin to race. It was early enough that most of Sage Gardens was still sound asleep. He wanted to make a quiet exit. He felt a pang of guilt for not telling Samantha the truth, but he wanted to make sure that she didn't get in the middle of what he was about to do.

As he drove towards Derek's house he thought

about everything that had happened. He hoped that he would be able to get all three arrested for the robbery, but he had to accept that he probably wouldn't be able to get them arrested for murder. He could only hope that the police would look into their involvement in the murder. He parked in the driveway and walked up to the front door. He placed his hand in his pocket to start the tape recorder. Just as he did Derek opened the door and startled Eddy. Eddy immediately withdrew his hand from his pocket. He wasn't sure if he had managed to start the recording and he didn't want to make Derek suspicious by putting his hand back in his pocket.

"So? Do you have some information for us?" Derek asked.

"Let's go inside first." Eddy gestured to the door.

Derek nodded and stepped back. Karl stood in the hallway inside the entrance. "Did you find out where the money is?" He looked at Eddy anxiously.

"I did." Eddy looked between the two men and knew that the next words he spoke would change everything.

"So?" Derek glared at him. "Where is it?"

"It's at a storage facility." The words left Eddy's mouth before he even realized he had decided to speak them.

"Let's go get it!" Derek started to open the door.

"Where are you going without me?" The door swung open hard behind Eddy. It struck him in the back. Eddy stumbled forward. When he caught himself and turned he found himself face to face with Charlie. "Did you think I was going to let any of you get away with this?" She pulled out her gun and closed the door behind her. "Did you think I wouldn't know about your little meetings?" She laughed as she waved the gun in their direction. "I know everything that you do."

"You don't trust us?" Derek did his best to seem tough.

"Trust you?" Charlie laughed again. "How could I trust someone that can't even make a simple murder look like an overdose?" Eddy was surprised as it didn't seem that Charlie pulled the trigger, but it did look like she had orchestrated it. He just hoped he was recording this.

"You're the one that decided to involve personal business and to get me to do your dirty work. None of it was necessary." Derek grimaced. "If I had known you were setting up someone you had a personal tie to, I wouldn't have done it."

"Don't try to pin this on me, Derek. Do you really think the police are just going to let that go?" She sighed. "I gave you a simple instruction. Leave some of the money, make it look like an overdose. The cops would assume he was the bank robber, and the entire thing would be over with. We would have been in the clear. Instead you messed everything up."

"You never told me he could fight." He pointed to the deep bruise on his cheek bone. "Do you think this felt good?" Eddy listened intently as he didn't want to interrupt them and stop them from telling the truth.

"Oh, toughen up." Charlie shook her head as she waved the gun. "None of it matters now, anyway."

"You're right it doesn't." Derek sneered. "All we want is our money."

"There was never going to be any sharing of the money, boys. Who cares if a parolee and a security guard who was an accomplice to a bank robbery end up dead? I can tell you who cares. Nobody." She chuckled and pointed the gun directly at Eddy. "And you? An old cop who decided to meddle? Well, you figured it out all right, and then the convicted criminal over here shot you. Sad story, but a simple story, and it's over." She shrugged. "I was going to wait a few more days, but since you two decided to go behind my back I had to move things up a little. Lucky enough for me, you all made it easy for me by being together. So, let's not drag this out." She pointed the gun at Derek. "Who are you going to shoot first?"

"What?" Derek stammered out. He took a few steps back. When Charlie waved the gun he froze.

"Oh, did you think I was going to do all of the dirty work? I had to clean up the mess you left with John, you fools, you couldn't even take care of that." She smirked.

"I had nothing to do with that," Karl protested. "I had nothing to do with the murder."

"Maybe not," Charlie said. "But the police are going to think otherwise."

"You don't have to do this," Derek said. Charlie waved the gun towards Derek in a threatening motion.

"Derek, if you don't want to pick, then you can be the first." She released the safety. "I respect the fact that you're man enough to volunteer."

"No wait, all right, I'll do it!" Derek gulped down a few breaths of air. "Eddy." He mumbled the name. Charlie pointed the gun at Eddy. Eddy braced himself. It wasn't until that moment when

Derek spoke his name that he realized he had gotten himself into a terrible situation. There wasn't much chance that he was going to get out of it. In the end Charlie was going to win. She was going to have all of the money. She was going to get away with arranging the murder of her ex-boyfriend. Terry and Paul might still be at risk. Eddy had sacrificed everything, for nothing.

"So, I guess you think you have it all settled then, Charlie?" Eddy was desperate to distract her. "But what you don't know is that Karl and Derek were planning on making you take the fall. In fact, I've contacted the police and they are on their way here now, to arrest you. You think you've won, but really, you're about to spend your life in prison."

"What?" Charlie snapped out the word. She continued to point the gun directly at Eddy, but she glared in Derek's direction.

"Don't listen to him!" Derek hissed. "He's making it all up. We would never turn you in."

"Never!" Karl glared at Eddy. "He's just mad

because Derek picked him to die."

"Fine, take the risk. You can waste your time trying to murder us all, or you can take your last chance to escape. It's your choice." Eddy tried to act casual.

Charlie flinched. It was the first time Eddy had seen her act anything but confident. All at once he was aware that she was terrified of going to jail. She wasn't afraid of violence, but she was afraid of handcuffs. He decided to apply a little pressure.

"The moment those sirens start flashing in the window, these two are going to trip over each other to be the first to turn you in. That's the consequence of being in charge, Charlie. The only thing that you can negotiate with is the money. If you can give the cops the missing money from the bank robbery, then you might be able to get your sentence reduced. But I can tell you right now, if you pull a trigger, you're not getting anything reduced." Eddy shook his head. "You'll be lucky if you get paroled in fifty years. Is that what you want?"

"You must really think I'm a fool." Charlie laughed. "I knew who you were from the moment I laid eyes on you. A real lone wolf. I don't believe for a second that you called for back-up. In fact I doubt that anyone even knows you're here. Do they?" She locked eyes with Eddy. "You don't have any back-up."

"Charlie, I can take care of him for you." Derek stepped forward. "Let me do it for you. I'll make sure nothing comes back on you. Just give me Karl's cut."

"Karl's cut?" Charlie grinned. "A little too late, Derek. I'm taking every last dime." She pointed the gun towards Derek. "Get against the wall or you'll be the first to go."

Derek glowered at her, but he did as she instructed. "You, against the other wall." She pointed the gun at Karl. Karl nervously moved towards the opposite wall. Eddy stood in the middle of both of them. His heart sank as he realized that his last hope had faded. Charlie was right. He hadn't listened to anyone. He had tried to do things on his own. Now he was going to pay the price. His only hope was that the tape recorder was recording and Charlie, Derek and Karl would be held accountable for their actions even if he wasn't around. Charlie turned her attention back to Eddy.

"Well, I guess it's now or never." Charlie pointed the gun at Eddy and started to pull back on the trigger.

"Drop the weapon!" The shout carried through the room with such force that Eddy jumped in response to it. It was not from either of the men beside him. It was from a man standing in the doorway. Detective Brunner had his gun aimed at Charlie. "Drop it now or I will shoot!"

Charlie stared hard into Eddy's eyes. The moment for her to flee had passed. The moment for her to shoot him had passed as well. There were no more options for her. She sighed and released her grip on the gun. The gun fell from her grasp and hit the ground beside her feet. Eddy sighed with relief. He stared at Detective Brunner as he walked up behind Charlie and pinned her arms behind her back. Behind him a few uniformed officers jogged up to the scene. They began taking Karl and Derek into custody.

"Don't you forget what I told you, Eddy, I'm a victim in all of this!" Karl wriggled his body in an attempt to escape the handcuffs.

"Oh, give it a rest, nobody believes you." Derek rolled his eyes. He submitted to the arrest as if it was a familiar act. "Just watch the wrists, all right? Last time the guy put the cuffs on too tight and it hurt for weeks."

The officer arresting him didn't seem too interested in being gentle.

"Are you okay, Eddy?" Detective Brunner turned to look at him with concern clear in his eyes. "Are you hurt?"

"No, I'm fine." Eddy was still amazed that the last person he would expect to save him did. "How did you know?"

"Later. Right now, we need to get these three into custody," Detective Brunner said. "Do you know who's responsible for what?"

"They were all involved in the robbery. Charlie just admitted to organizing the murder, but Derek pulled the trigger. I think you'll find that John Baker had nothing to do with the robbery. He was used as a fall guy and was murdered because of his personal ties to Charlie," Eddy said as he slowly pulled the tape recorder out of his pocket. He looked down at it and sighed with relief as he stopped the recording. "This will explain it all," Eddy said as he handed it to Detective Brunner.

"Old school." Detective Brunner nodded.

"Always the best." Eddy smiled. "The money. The money is at a storage facility across town." He saw Charlie flinch as she was lead out of the house by the officers. She had overheard Eddy mention the storage facility and he knew that he was right, the money was there. "Now Detective Brunner, your case can be closed. Please, make sure these criminals get the justice that they deserve."

"Not just yet." Detective Brunner grimaced and looked away from Eddy.

"What do you mean?" Eddy narrowed his eyes. He wondered if he had missed something important. He couldn't have gone to all of this trouble only to have everything fall apart. "Don't you have all of the proof that you need?"

"Oh sure. Along with the confessions that I'm sure we'll get when they try to pin everything on each other."

"Then what is the problem? Why can't you close the case?" Eddy frowned.

"The paperwork, Eddy. There's always the paperwork." Detective Brunner hung his head. "It's going to be hell explaining this one."

Eddy chuckled and nodded. "I don't miss the paperwork."

"Nobody does." Detective Brunner grinned.

As Eddy looked into the young detective's eyes he felt a pang of remorse for ever doubting him. Maybe he didn't do things the way Eddy would have, but in the end he had arrived just in time.

"Apparently, there's a mole in the department that's been feeding information to Derek."

"Really," Detective Brunner said thoughtfully. "I have a feeling I know who that is. They are being investigated by Internal Affairs at the moment. I'll have to pass that information on to the relevant people for them to look into."

"Do you mind if I get some air?" Eddy pointed to the door.

"Feel free, just don't go far. The fresher the information, the better."

"I won't."

Eddy walked out of the house and sighed with relief at the fresh air. As he walked towards the curb, he began to get an inkling of what had saved his life. Samantha stood beside one of the patrol cars. As soon as she saw him she stood up and ran towards him.

"Eddy! You're okay!" She gazed at him with relief. "They told me I had to wait out here. I didn't want to. But Detective Brunner threatened to cuff me." She scowled.

"I'm okay." He smiled at her. "Thanks to Detective Brunner showing up at just the right time. I wonder how he managed that." He raised an eyebrow and looked into her eyes.

"I called him." Samantha frowned as if she expected him to be angry. "I knew you didn't want me to, but I was concerned and my gut instinct told me I could trust him. Sometimes, Eddy you forget that not having a badge can make a big difference, and not having back-up can make an even bigger difference. I knew that you would come here, even when you said you wouldn't."

"Maybe it was risky, but I felt like I had to do it."

"What? Walking into a den of thieves and murderers with the purpose of agitating them," Samantha pointed out with a grim smile. "A bit risky?"

"Okay, a lot risky." Eddy smiled. "But it all worked out in the end. Charlie admitted to arranging for Derek to kill John and Derek admitted to doing it. So, they should go down for the murder as well as the robbery."

"That's a relief." Samantha smiled. "Good work, Eddy."

"Thanks to all of us," Eddy said. Eddy looked around to make sure no one could hear him. "I also found out that Terry was being blackmailed by Karl because she worked out he was involved in the robbery, but I'll tell you the whole story later."

"Ooh, I can't wait," she said enthusiastically. "That was certainly the most adventurous birthday present I've ever received."

"I didn't expect it to get quite so adventurous." Eddy laughed. "How did you get Detective Brunner here?"

"I called to tell him we had found the floorplan and the gloves and he agreed to send a car over to check. I had no idea that he was going himself."

"Apparently, he trusted my instincts." Eddy smiled.

"And mine." Samantha gave him a quick hug. "I'm just glad that you're safe, Eddy. You know that you mean a lot to all of us. We need you to be safe."

"I appreciate that, Samantha. I have to say that if we hadn't all worked as a team I don't think we would have been able to pull this off. It's good to know that if there's ever trouble in Sage Gardens I have plenty of back-up."

"Absolutely." She smiled at him. "Never forget that, Eddy."

The End

More Cozy Mysteries by Cindy Bell

Dune House Cozy Mysteries

Seaside Secrets

Boats and Bad Guys

Treasured History

Hidden Hideaways

Dodgy Dealings

Suspects and Surprises

Heavenly Highland Inn Cozy Mysteries

Murdering the Roses

Dead in the Daisies

Killing the Carnations

Drowning the Daffodils

Suffocating the Sunflowers

Books, Bullets and Blooms

A Deadly serious Gardening Contest

A Bridal Bouquet and a Body

Wendy the Wedding Planner Cozy Mysteries

Matrimony, Money and Murder

Chefs, Ceremonies and Crimes

Knives and Nuptials

Mice, Marriage and Murder

Bekki the Beautician Cozy Mysteries

Hairspray and Homicide

A Dyed Blonde and a Dead Body

Mascara and Murder

Pageant and Poison

Conditioner and a Corpse

Mistletoe, Makeup and Murder

Hairpin, Hair Dryer and Homicide

Blush, a Bride and a Body

Shampoo and a Stiff

Cosmetics, a Cruise and a Killer

Lipstick, a Long Iron and Lifeless

Camping, Concealer and Criminals

Treated and Dyed